Praise for

"A fun mystery series that's a sure bet for animal lovers."
—*School Library Journal*

"This first book in a new series is definitely for the animal-lover, and the Scooby-Doo vibe makes it a perfect fit for the budding mystery fan. Young readers will enjoy following the clues along with Kelsey as she learns about friendship and animals."—*Booklist*

"There's plenty of action in this series opener, but Singleton also handles the emotional layers well. Pet lovers will enjoy the animal-centric focus, and the mystery will keep them guessing."—*Publishers Weekly*

"This enjoyable mystery has a satisfying ending and a neatly calibrated level of suspense."—*Kirkus Reviews*

"This is a feel-good book with a myriad of unexpected twists, turns, and surprises."—*VOYA*

"Ultimately as fuzzy and accessible as a kitten chasing a ball of string, this story—and subsequent titles in the series—will likely find a ready audience among animal lovers, amateur sleuths, and the fairly common combination of the two."
—*Bulletin of the Center for Children's Books*

The Curious Cat Spy Club Mysteries

Book Three
Kelsey the Spy

Linda Joy Singleton

Albert Whitman & Company
Chicago, Illinois

To Nikoli, Patrick, and Breonna and Mom-Dad

With thanks to tortoise expert Abigail DeSesa
from the California Turtle & Tortoise Club

And in memory of Louise Fitzhugh, the author
of *Harriet the Spy*, who inspired me as a child
to write journals and spy with my best friend.

Library of Congress Cataloging-in-Publication data
is on file with the publisher.

Text copyright © 2016 by Linda Joy Singleton
Cover illustration © 2016 by Kristi Valiant
Interior illustrations and hand lettering by Jordan Kost
Hardcover edition published in 2016 by Albert Whitman & Company
Paperback edition published in 2016 by Albert Whitman & Company
ISBN 978-0-8075-1384-2

Printed in the United States of America
10 9 8 7 6 5 4 3 2 1 LB 24 23 22 21 20 19 18 17 16

Design by Ellen Kokontis

For more information about Albert Whitman & Company,
visit our web site at www.albertwhitman.com.

Contents

- Chapter 1 -
Follow That Suspect!

My brother gets a phone call during breakfast. A guilty look crosses his face, and I know he has a secret.

"Got to go!" Kyle shoves his phone into his pocket as he jumps up from the table.

"But I'm making you another crepe Benedict." Dad frowns at Kyle. Chef Dad takes his cooking very seriously.

"Give it to Kelsey." My brother is already dumping his dirty plate and silverware in the sink. "A friend needs my help."

I study my brother, suspicious. Since we lost our house and moved into this apartment, all Kyle does is apply for college scholarships and study, study, study. He has zero social life.

"What friend?" I ask him.

"My buddy Jake really needs my help with, um, some heavy lifting. You remember him from our old neighborhood?"

Oh, I remember him all right. I also remember the distinctive ringtone Kyle assigned to Jake's number—a blaring disaster alert. But the ringtone I just heard was music. Either Kyle changed the ringtone or he's lying. I sense a big whopper of a lie. I don't know who called Kyle, but it wasn't his buddy Jake.

So I do what any spy would do.

I follow him.

Unfortunately I only take a few steps before Dad's voice stops me.

"Kelsey, are you leaving too?" He sounds hurt. "Aren't you going to finish your crepe?"

Drats. I've insulted Dad's culinary pride. Before Café Belmond closed, he was known as the best baker in Sun Flower. Now he can't find a job and is home way too much.

"The crepe was delicious," I say. "It's just that I have to—"

My brain goes blank. *I have to…*

Seriously, a good spy needs to create a believable

story in a split-second. And Dad is staring at me the same way I just stared at Kyle: full-on suspicious. I can't use school as an excuse because it's Saturday. I can't say I'm full because I didn't finish eating my crepe. The only reason Kyle got away so easily was because he'd already devoured four crepes.

"I'm late for a meeting at Becca's house." This isn't a lie. Leo sent a message saying he solved a mystery. (What mystery? I have no idea—it's a mystery to me!) He asked Becca and me to meet him at noon at the Skunk Shack. That's more than two hours from now, but a half-truth is more believable than a total lie.

"What sort of meeting?" Dad asks.

This is where belonging to a top-secret club gets tricky because I can't tell Dad about the Curious Cat Spy Club. Becca, Leo, and I started the CCSC to care for three rescued kittens. While our families know we're friends, they don't know we help animals by finding lost pets and solving mysteries.

But I can talk about the Sparklers, a school volunteer group that Becca belongs to. I touch the silver crescent-moon necklace that the Sparklers loaned me since I'm helping them plan a booth for the Humane Society fund-raiser.

"Becca and I are meeting to discuss ideas for the Sparkler booth," I tell Dad.

"She can wait until you finish your breakfast." He gestures to my plate. "Another ten minutes won't matter."

But in ten minutes Kyle could be gone.

When all else fails, resort to bodily functions.

"I have to go..." I shift anxiously and glance down. "You know...*go*."

"Oh." He nods, understanding. "Well, don't let me keep you."

Before he can say any more, I'm out of the kitchen.

I don't go farther than my brother's room, where I hear hurried footsteps and banging drawers. When the footsteps move my way, I dash across the hall and duck into the bathroom.

Cracking the door open, I spy on Kyle. Slowly, his door opens. He looks furtively up and down the hall, then steps out holding a large, white rectangular box.

What's in the box? It can't be very heavy or breakable since he tucks it under one arm before hurrying down the hall.

He's definitely up to something sneaky, and I'm going to find out what it is.

I wait until he's out of sight then rush into my room. I push a stool to the closet and climb up to grab the hidden green backpack. Slipping my spy pack over my shoulders, I race out of the apartment in pursuit of my brother.

A chilly wind, much too cold for early April in California, slaps my face and tosses my long hair into tangles. Should I go back for my jacket? No time. A glance over the second-floor railing shows Kyle at the bike rack strapping the large box onto his bike.

He jumps on his bike and rides off.

I run downstairs and hop on my bike to follow my brother.

My suspicions are confirmed when he doesn't make a right toward our old neighborhood where Jake lives, but a left toward downtown Sun Flower.

It's easy keeping up with Kyle, especially after he pulls over to adjust the straps holding the box to his bike. Also, he's big on obeying rules so he stops at every intersection, even when there's no stop sign.

Kyle is such a Percy, I think, remembering the sleepover when I played a game matching family members to Harry Potter characters with friends from my old neighborhood. My twin sisters are obviously the Patel twins. Dad with his cooking passion and high emotions is Mrs. Weasley. I couldn't decide on Mom since she's an animal lover like Hagrid and obsessed with gardening like Professor Sprout. But Kyle is definitely arrogant overachiever Percy.

I chose Luna for myself, but as I bike past familiar homes and businesses, I feel more like a character from my favorite book, *Harriet the Spy*.

I love the scenes when Harriet bikes on her spy route, jotting down what her neighbors are doing in her notebook. I keep a notebook too, not about what people are doing, but the secrets they hide. Becca knows I collect secrets, but I've never shown my notebook of secrets to her or anyone. Like Harriet's, my notebook is for my eyes only.

At a stop sign, my brother glances over his shoulder. Quickly, I duck behind a parked truck. *Whew!* He almost saw me. To be safe, I stay about a block behind him, keeping him in sight but not close enough to be noticed.

We're pedaling now through downtown Sun Flower, which isn't very big, just a few blocks of businesses. Kyle makes a left into a U-shaped mini mall. I pick up my speed, but when I roll into the parking lot, Kyle is gone.

Where did he go?

Straddling my bike seat, I peer up and down the mini mall. The entrance and exit open on this street, so Kyle has to be here. But I don't see him or his bike. Did he go into one of the businesses? Paul's Pawn Shop, Legal Eagle Associates, Friendly's Café, and Prehistoric Pizza are dark with closed signs. The only business open this early on a weekend is the sheriff's office.

I met Sheriff Fischer when the CCSC rescued stolen pets and helped a lost zorse. Sheriff Fischer is cool and doesn't talk down to kids. He's also a friend of Becca's mother. I don't see his official car in the parking lot, so he's probably out on patrol. There's no reason for Kyle to go into the sheriff's office. But the other businesses are closed, so where did he go?

Biting my lip, I can't decide what to do—until I spot a shadowed alley hidden between the pawn-shop and the pizza place. Pedaling over, I stare into the dank-smelling tunnel of darkness. It's empty except for scattered trash and garbage cans. I unzip my spy pack and take out my flash cap. The tiny but powerful beam lights my way as I ride through the alley to a street behind the mall. There's no sign of my brother, only a few parked semis and vacant lots on a dead-end street.

Did Kyle know I was following him and purposely lose me?

He's long gone by now—and I didn't discover his secret.

It's too early to meet the club at the Skunk Shack, but I don't want to bike all the way back home. I'm close to Leo's house, and if I go there, we can ride to Becca's together. He might show me his latest robotic inventions. Leo's mechanical dragon drone and key spider are amazing. Also, I'm curious about the mystery he says he solved.

Coasting my bike into Leo's driveway is like leaving spring for winter. Everything is snowy white: the house, rocks decorating the yard, and lacy window curtains. His mother is obsessed with cleanliness, requiring guests to take off their shoes and use a sanitizer dispenser by the door. I wipe my sweaty hands on my jeans, smooth back my tangled honey-brown curls, and push the doorbell.

No one answers. But I know Mrs. Polanski is home because her car, a white Sorento, is parked in the driveway. I press the doorbell again.

And I wait.

A career as a spy requires a lot of waiting. Surveillance is just another word for waiting, and it takes a lot of patience. Piecing together clues and gathering evidence takes time too. But sometimes I get impatient.

If I had a cell phone, I could text Leo to find out where he is. But my parents can't afford phones for all four kids—and the youngest (me) is last in line.

As I try the doorbell again, I press my ear against the door to make sure the bell works. Yup, the muffled *ding-dong* echoes through the house. Yet no one shows up.

Sighing, I head back to my bike.

I'm grabbing my handlebars when the wind carries the sound of voices. Curious, I look around but don't see anyone. I cup my ear, listening. The voices come from the backyard.

Decorative flower-shaped pavers wind toward the backyard gate. Crouching down, I peek through a gap in the gate. Leo's mother is sipping tea with another woman at a white wicker table. The other woman has blond hair piled high on her head and wide blue eyes set in an oval face like Leo's mother. I suspect they're sisters.

"So tell me about the surprise," the other woman says, lifting her porcelain teacup to her frosted red lips.

Surprise? The word draws my curiosity like a magnet, and of course, I listen. It's what I do best.

"Leo has no idea." Mrs. Polanski chuckles.

"It'll be hard to keep anything from my clever nephew." My suspicion was right. She's Leo's aunt.

"Not this time," Mrs. Polanski says confidently. "Although Leo usually figures out my plans before I've made them. Like last summer when I tried to surprise him with a weekend at the beach, but somehow he knew and had covered himself with sunscreen. And when I told him we were going to Lake Tahoe a few months ago, he already had his ski clothes packed. It's hard to surprise a smart kid like Leo. But he'll never guess what I'm planning for his birthday."

Leo is having a birthday? I think, startled. Leo never once mentioned his birthday. I don't even know the date.

A blond curl dangles from Leo's aunt's hair tower as she leans closer. "What are you planning?"

Mrs. Polanski grins. "A surprise birthday bash."

"With other children?" Leo's aunt sounds shocked. "But Leopold is such a loner."

"Not anymore. He's made some friends at school," Mrs. Polanski says proudly. "I worried when his only friends were robots."

"That's wonderful he has some little friends," the aunt says.

Little friends? I roll my eyes. *Seriously, does she think we're still in kindergarten?*

"I worry about him though," Mrs. Polanski adds, frowning. "Celebrating his birthday is risky. What if his friends discover his secret?"

Logical, scientific, honest Leo has a secret? Something to do with birthdays? Could he have an allergy to birthday cake? A phobia of balloons? A tragically sick twin who's hidden away from the world?

"I don't know what to do." Mrs. Polanski pushes away her teacup. "Keeping the pretense was easy when Leo didn't have friends. But now something as simple as a cake or a birthday card could expose the lie."

"He should tell his friends the truth."

"I've begged him to." Mrs. Polanski sighs. "But Leo refuses."

Her sister shrugs. "It's just a number."

"A number is a big deal in middle school." Mrs. Polanski wrings her hands. "But I don't want to risk Leo being hurt. So at his birthday party, I'll put thirteen candles on the cake. Leo's friends must never know he's only turning twelve."

- Chapter 2 -
Suspicions

I stagger away from the gate, so shocked I trip over a paver stone. I don't feel any pain, only numbness as I pick myself up and jump on my bike. Even if Leo is home, I can't talk to him right now. The words I just heard don't compute.

How can brilliant Leo—our club's covert technology strategist—be two years younger than me? Eleven years old!

To be fair, I turned thirteen in March so he's probably only a year and a couple months younger. But OMG—he's the age I was in elementary school. How can he act so mature and spout off knowledge like a miniature teacher when he's barely in double digits?

Calm down and think this through, I tell myself as I pedal away.

It's not like being younger is a crime. I can even guess how this happened. Leo is supersmart, which really impresses teachers, so he must have skipped a grade. All this time, I thought Leo was short for his age like me. But he's the average height for a sixth grader.

I don't consciously decide to go to Becca's house, but that's where my bike is headed. I have to tell Becca. No, I can't tell her. That wouldn't be fair to Leo. Yet how can I keep something this huge from Becca?

There's a saying that people who eavesdrop hear terrible things about themselves. But hearing something shocking about a friend is worse. Protecting one friend means lying to another. I understand how Leo's mother feels, torn between truth and lies. We're stuck in the same boat and floating without paddles.

I wish I could unknow Leo's secret.

When I roll through the entry gate into Wild Oaks Sanctuary, a flock of peacocks crossing the road shriek and flutter shimmery feathers, then fly into the trees. It's still too early to meet at the Skunk Shack so I ride up to Becca's house. I hope she's inside and not helping her mother care for rescued animals somewhere on their fifty-six-acre sanctuary. Becca could be in the pasture, the barn, or one of the many animal enclosures.

Before I even step on the porch, the front door opens and Becca bursts out. "Kelsey! What a great surprise!"

Surprise. Not my favorite word right now. I cringe but Becca doesn't seem to notice. "Is it okay to come early?" I ask.

"Way okay!" She grasps my arm and pulls me into her house. "You're rescuing me from a severe case of boredom. Mom's out to brunch with a friend and won't be back for hours. Let's go hang out in my room." Becca's face lights up with a smile so genuine that I want to tell her everything.

"I found out something," I say, trying to sound mysterious. "It's about—"

"Watch out!" Becca interrupts as an orange streak races through her legs and into the kitchen.

"Hey, that's my kitten!" I stare toward the kitchen where I hear scampering paws. "What's Honey running from?"

I get my answer when a whirl of black whooshes by my ankles.

"And there goes my kitten in pursuit." Becca laughs.

"Why are Honey and Chris running loose in the house? I thought they were staying in the back room."

"Like that lasted long. Mom and I are softies," Becca admits. "They meowed until Mom and I let them in the kitchen, then the living room, and now they have the run of the house—literally. Hey, don't climb on the table!"

Becca rushes off in pursuit of Chris who is chasing Honey. It's like watching an animal channel sitcom, and I burst out laughing.

When Honey darts in my direction, I grab her and cradle my sweet fur-baby in my arms. Her purr rumbles like kitty music. Becca finally catches Chris, and we take our kittens into her bedroom.

Every time I enter Becca's room, I feel like I'm upside down. Bookcases aren't on the floor but hung high on the wall near the ceiling. Pictures and drawings cover the ceiling like wallpaper. Only Becca's bed, a dresser, and a chair are on the floor. A rolling ladder leans near a high bulletin board covered with notes and photos. Becca designed her room so it's animal proof because she shares it with a menagerie, and teachers are skeptical of excuses like, "A goat ate my textbook." Since the nights have been warmer, the goat prefers the pasture, but two dogs jump off the bed to greet us.

My kitten isn't used to dogs yet and hisses. But the dogs are too busy tail-wagging to notice. She'll have to get used to them, because my family has a fabulous golden-whip (golden retriever plus whippet) named Handsome. Unfortunately, due to the no-pets rule in our apartment, Handsome is living with my grandmother for now. But I hope we'll be living together again eventually.

Becca flops on her bed, patting the larger dog with one hand and plopping the smaller dog on her lap. She turns to me. "So what were you saying? You found out something?"

"Did I ever! I'm still in shock." I pull up the chair and sink onto the hard seat. "It doesn't really matter...It's just hard to believe that he..." I shake my head.

"Go on," Becca urges with a flick of her hand. "Who did what?"

The words are like grenades ready to explode if I don't say them. But my mouth dries up. Leo's secret isn't mine to share. As much as I want to tell

Becca, it feels wrong. She's staring at me, leaning forward like she's poised to catch whatever I toss at her. I have to tell her something.

"It's about...about my brother." I shift my thoughts in a new direction. "He was acting suspicious at breakfast and carrying a mysterious box, so I followed him."

Becca strokes the little dog in her lap as I talk, never taking her gaze off me. When I get to the part where Kyle bikes down the shadowed alley and vanishes, her eyes spark with curiosity.

"Any idea where he went?" she asks.

"Nope," I answer. "But I think he was delivering something in the box."

"I know! He went to the sheriff's office to report a crime." Becca taps her purple-tipped fingernail on her chin. "And the box contained evidence."

I consider this, then shake my head. "I doubt it. Kyle only leaves the house for school or the library."

"But you don't know that for sure. Did you check inside the sheriff's office?"

"No."

"Well, you should have."

Becca's right. I assumed my brother went somewhere else, so I didn't investigate. What kind of spy gives up so easily? Like the book *Spy Now, Die Later* says, "Assumptions are roadblocks to discoveries." I have to stop making assumptions or I'll never discover anything.

"I bet something supersecret was in the box." Becca twirls the end of her long ponytail. "Maybe your brother is a courier for the CIA."

I laugh. "Kyle's not that interesting."

"But he's up to something sneaky." Becca shifts so she's sitting cross-legged.

"I'm sure of it," I agree. "I'll keep a close eye on him and try to search his room. If he still has the box, I'll find out what's inside."

We try to guess what could be in the box (jewels? money? love letters?), and then we discuss ideas for the Sparkler booth. The Humane Society fundraiser is just a week away, so we have to work fast. "We have plenty of ideas," I say. "The problem is getting five girls to agree on one—"

"Especially when one of the girls is Tyla." Becca slumps against a pillow. "Tyla's so sure her ideas are the best—even when they aren't—that it's hard to tell her no. And usually I get stuck with the work because the others are too busy. That's why I wanted you in our group, even if it's only for a week."

"I'm not into sparkly stuff, but I'm all for helping the Humane Society."

"I hope we can come up with a fabulous idea. If not, Tyla will get her way and we'll have a face-painting booth." Becca groans. "Again."

We brainstorm great ideas and terrible ideas—popping balloons, fishing for prizes, karaoke, beanbag toss, fortune-telling—until Becca remembers she has to go check on a bear cub named Fuzzy Wuzzy. The poor orphaned cub was found wandering alone with burn scars after a forest fire.

I love walking with Becca through the sanctuary, surrounded by so many amazing animals. After I help her feed the bear cub, I pet a fawn and cuddle long-haired bunnies. The only creature I avoid is the alligator that snaps loudly when we walk by his enclosure.

At almost noon, we climb the path to meet Leo.

The Skunk Shack, our CCSC clubhouse, is hidden by overgrown bushes and towering trees on Becca's hilly property. We cared for the kittens here until Leo took his kitten home and Becca moved our two into her house. More than anything, I wish I could take Honey home, but I can't while we're living in an apartment that doesn't allow pets.

Leo is already inside the Skunk Shack, reaching high to polish the glassy face of the grandfather clock. When we fixed up this shack, we were surprised to find the broken clock in jumbled pieces. Leo was determined to repair it, and he's done an amazing job. A brass pendulum swings behind a glass box, and the clock chimes on the hour. But it's still a mystery why a grandfather clock was left in a shack once used for stinky animals. The only clue we have is an old black-and-white photograph of a little boy riding a tortoise.

"Nine, eight, seven, six..." Leo counts down. "Listen for it!"

The grandfather clock starts to chime, a sweet sound that echoes in our clubhouse. I'm not watching the clock though; I'm studying Leo. When we first met, I thought he was arrogant, stubborn, and annoying. He is—but I quickly learned he's also clever, kind, and loyal. Now we're good friends.

How can he be only eleven? He talks like a dictionary and wears formal slacks with a button-down shirt under a vest like a teacher. But when the clock chimes for the twelfth time, he breaks into a boyish grin that shows his true age.

His secret, I remind myself and shove it to the

back of my mind.

"Leo, I stopped by your house a few hours ago, but no one answered the door." I pull out my chair from our table and sit so I'm facing Leo. "Where were you?"

"I was with Frankie." Leo sits too, his posture straight and his head held high. "We were calculating variances of movement and adjusting gears on a warthog."

Becca looks up from where she's sorting through our snack box, her black brows arched. "A warthog?"

"A mechanical version of the fictional character from the *Lion King*."

"Oh, for the drama club," Becca says.

I nod, understanding. Frankie is Leo's new friend. Leo met Frankie, the set designer for the school drama club, when we were searching for a zorse's mask. Since then Leo has been skipping club meetings to help Frankie.

"It's abnormal for Mom not to answer the door." Leo taps his finger to his chin thoughtfully. "She and Aunt Joanne may have gone shopping."

Or into the backyard to share tea and secrets, I think.

Leo tilts his head at me. "Why did you come over?"

"I was following a suspect." I smile mysteriously. "But I lost him near your house so I stopped by to see you."

His blond brows rise. "What suspect?"

"First tell us why you called this meeting," I counter. "Your email was very cryptic."

"What mystery did you solve, Leo?" Becca asks as she rips into a bag of apple chips.

"All will be revealed in due course."

"Tell us now," I demand, leaning forward in my chair.

Leo ignores me. He thuds his fist on the table. "I hereby call our CCSC meeting to order."

"I second that," Becca and I say at the same time to hurry him up.

Leo gives his detailed (and boring) treasurer's report. We've received reward money for returning lost pets, which pays for kitten supplies like food and litter. We haven't spent much lately so our treasury is looking good.

Next is old business, and Leo gets an excited gleam in his blue eyes. "I solved a cryptic clue."

He reaches into his pocket and pulls out the old photo he found in the grandfather clock.

I've seen the photo before, but it's really cool so I look again. The boy is about three years old with either black or brown hair; it's impossible to tell in a black-and-white photo. He wears old-fashioned suspenders, dark shoes, and pleated slacks. And he's riding a giant tortoise.

"According to my research, this tortoise is an Aldabra, the world's second-largest tortoise species," Leo says in his usual know-it-all way. "Aldabra tortoises can live over two hundred years. At first I thought this photo was from the 1800s because 1897 was scribbled on the back. But I was wrong."

"You? Wrong?" I can't resist teasing.

"It's a rare occurrence," he admits in total seriousness. "But 1897 isn't a date. The clothing and photo paper prove the picture was taken in the 1950s."

Becca plops an apple chip in her mouth. "So what do the numbers mean?"

"I considered a phone number, because back then some phone numbers only had four digits with a location like Lincoln-5641," Leo says as he crosses the room to get a magnifying glass from his toolbox. He holds the glass over the photo so Becca and I can get a closer look. "Only the numeral sequence didn't correlate. Notice the space before the seven and the smudge afterward like faded writing? Under microscope examination, that smudge turned out to be the letters *s* and *t*."

"The abbreviation for street," Becca guesses.

"Affirmative." Leo nods. "I checked a map, and 189 Seventh Street is a real address. It's 1.3 miles from our current location."

"That's great!" I jump off my chair. "Someone there might know about the grandfather clock."

"And the tortoise," Becca adds.

"What are we waiting for?" Leo is already across the room and opening the door. "Let's go sleuthing."

Chapter 3

The Long Secret

Leo hops on his robotic gyro-board, clicks the remote control, and zooms off. Becca and I have to pedal our bikes fast to keep up.

As I bump down the dirt trail, I inhale crisp piney air, feeling excited and lucky to be in the CCSC. Becca, Leo, and I never would have become friends if we hadn't rescued the kittens from a dumpster. Since then we've solved two mysteries, and if we find out who left the grandfather clock in our shack, that will make three.

We leave the rustic woods for a paved road, then coast downhill into downtown Sun Flower. There are only three streets of businesses surrounded by older neighborhoods. After a few turns, we're on Seventh

Street where single-storied houses all have the same L-shaped design—except for the towering home at 189 Seventh Street. It looks like a mini-castle with stone walls, turrets, green hedges, and cobbled paths circling a pond with a stone frog fountain.

"I always wondered about this house." Becca stares up in awe. "Whenever I ride by, I imagine there's a princess trapped inside the turret."

"Kidnapped by a fire-breathing dragon who is really an enchanted prince," I say, playing along.

"The princess's kiss will turn him into a prince," Becca adds, "but his fire breath could kill her, and he loves her too much to risk her life."

I sigh. "Poor dragon."

Leo looks at us like we're crazy. "It's physically impossible for a reptile to breathe fire," he says. "And a dragon is a mythological creature."

"But dragons are cool," I say, winking at Becca. I spin my bike around and point down the block to a street corner with a bench. "Let's get to spying. That bus stop will make a good stakeout location."

"I didn't bring my surveillance drones," Leo says. "But my phone has a spy app with flashlight, sonic alert, voice disguise, zoom cam, and voice recorder."

"I have my spy pack." I reach up to pat my back-pack. "I've added disguises—a wig, a hat, dark glasses, and a fake mustache."

"A mustache would look a little silly on me." Becca giggles as she puts her finger under her nose to demonstrate. "And Leo is too young for facial hair."

Younger than you know, I think.

"Disguises are useful surveillance tools." Leo nods at me approvingly. "We may have to wait all day for someone to enter or exit the house."

"Or we could knock on the door and ask about the photo," Becca suggests.

I grin. "That could work too."

We park our bikes in the driveway, then follow the cobbled path around the frog fountain and up the steep front steps. Instead of a doorbell, there's a dragon-head door knocker.

"A dragon guards the door," Becca teases, then thuds the door knocker.

I draw back, almost expecting a fiery roar, but nothing happens...until the door opens.

Standing in front of us is a movie-star gorgeous guy. He's college-aged and looks familiar. When he smiles, his teeth are white enough to sell toothpaste.

"May I help you?" he asks in a British accent.

I glance over at Becca, expecting her to do the talking since she's our club's social operative. But she's staring like she's been hypnotized.

I must be staring too, because it's Leo who speaks up.

"Good afternoon," he says with a formal nod. "I'm Leopold, and these are my friends Kelsey and Becca."

"My mates call me Reggie. I do hope you're selling something edible. My cupboards are quite bare." He looks at my backpack hopefully. "Do you have biscuits, I mean, cookies?"

"Sorry." I shake my head. "We're not selling anything."

"My bad luck," Reggie says lightly. "So what can I do for you?"

Becca snaps out of her trance and flashes a sweet smile. "We'd just like to ask you a few questions. We're doing a school project on—"

"Unique architecture," Leo says.

"And we're interested in your house," I finish.

"Happy to oblige," Reggie says cheerfully. "Go on."

I zip open my spy pack and take out a notebook, a pen, and a granola bar. "Here, this should help your hunger." I offer him the granola bar. "I hope you like peanut-butter caramel."

"My new favorite food," he says, ripping off the wrapping.

"Your house is amazing—like a suburban castle." I flip open the notebook official-like. "When was it built?"

"Let me think…" He gulps down half of the granola bar in one bite. "1957."

I jot this down in my notebook. "How long have you lived here?"

"Ten years," Reggie says.

Drats. That's not long enough to know about our photo. I'm ready to give up, but Becca steps forward.

"Do you know who lived here before you?" she asks.

"I certainly do." Reggie nods. "My granddad built this house. He's gone now, and Grandmum lives in Arizona. You'd do better to interview her. I don't know much about architecture."

"Do you know about this?" Leo reaches into his pocket and pulls out the boy-with-tortoise photograph.

"Blimey, it's Granddad. My sister's youngest boy is the spitting image of him." Reggie pushes back his hair as he leans in for a closer look. "Where in the world did you get this?"

"Inside a clock," Leo says. "It slipped out when the clock chimed."

Reggie gasps. "Not a grandfather clock?"

"How did you know?" Leo's blond brows arch like question marks.

"I haven't seen the clock since I was a child, but I've always wondered what happened to it. I don't know if I'm more astonished that you found this photo or that you got Grandfather's blasted clock to work properly."

"It was a challenge," Leo admits. "The clock was dismantled and had more broken parts than working ones."

"But Leo put it back together." Becca gestures proudly at Leo and he blushes. "We found it in an old shack on my property. Any idea how it got there?"

"I do indeed," Reggie surprises me by saying. "Regretfully, I can't tell you because it's a dusty skeleton in my family closet, and the truth would hurt people I love."

"Keeping secrets isn't easy," I say, my spy pack heavy on my shoulders.

"But won't you tell us, please?" Becca asks in a

cajoling voice. "Leo worked so hard to fix the clock, and we're dying of curiosity. We won't tell anyone."

"The margin of risk is slim since we don't know your family," Leo adds.

"We'll cross our hearts and promise to keep your secret." I make a solemn cross gesture over my heart. "We just want to know how the grandfather clock ended up in an old shack."

"And why the boy—your grandfather—was riding a turtle," Becca says.

"Not a turtle," Mr. Know-It-All Leo corrects. "An Aldabra tortoise."

"A tortoise is still a turtle," Becca argues.

"You're both right." Reggie nods approvingly. "Contrary to popular belief, tortoises are turtles rather than a separate group. The tortoise in this photo is an *Aldabrachelys gigantea*—commonly known as an Aldabra."

"I've only seen them in zoos." Becca's voice rises with her passion for animals. "My mom runs Wild Oaks Sanctuary, and we've had box turtles but never a giant tortoise."

"Renee Morales is your mother?" Reggie asks, surprised.

"You know Mom?" Becca's ponytail dangles over

her shoulder as she leans forward.

"I saw her in a TV interview about Wild Oaks Sanctuary and called for information on becoming a volunteer. She set up an appointment for me, but I got a call back for a commercial and had to cancel. I have mad respect for the work your mother does at Wild Oaks. I'm all for helping animals."

"We are too," I say with a fond look at my club mates.

"I'm amazed that you tracked me down from just an old photo." He rubs his stubbly chin thoughtfully as he stares at us. "You kids worked so hard that you deserve to know the whole story. I'm a good judge of character and feel I can trust you with a secret I've kept for a long time. Here's what really happened to my grandfather's grandfather clock..."

- Chapter 4 -
Mystery Solved

A short time later, we're sitting on stone benches beside a stone fountain, water spilling from a big-mouthed frog. Reggie offers us glasses of root beer bubbling with scoops of vanilla ice cream.

"My cupboards are bare but I found ice cream in the freezer. Nothing better than a root beer float on a crisp spring day," Reggie says in his lilting accent. "I'll start my story with some family history."

Becca, Leo, and I lean on the edge of the bench to face Reggie. A cool breeze swirls around us, as if it's listening for secrets too.

"As a child, I didn't see my grandparents often because I lived in England and they were here in Sun Flower," Reggie says, clasping his frosty glass. "But a decade ago, my parents, sister, and I moved here because Granddad was ill. After he died, Grandmum moved to a senior community in Arizona. My parents stayed here because we're quite big on tradition so it was important to keep the house in the family." He wipes off ice cream that drips down the side of his frothy glass and licks his fingers. "Grandmum's apartment is much smaller than this house so she left furniture behind—including Granddad's grandfather clock."

Becca's brows arch. "The one we found?"

"Yes. My father was thrilled to own the clock but couldn't get the chimes to work. Determined to fix the clock, he spread out the pieces on the kitchen table and worked on it for days, then months. The clock became an obsession." Reggie sighs. "Mum complained she couldn't use her kitchen. This led to an awful row—"

"Row?" Becca interrupts.

"An argument," Reggie explains. "Mum threatened to leave Dad and take my sister and me back to England if Dad didn't get rid of the clock. But Dad refused."

"Oh no," Becca cries. "What happened?"

"Evaline—my clever, dramatic sister—came up

with a plan." He grins wickedly. "And as her loyal younger brother, I went along with her."

Reggie sips his root beer float, then wipes away the foamy mustache. I feel moisture on my own lips and lick them.

"It was past midnight when Ev and I crept into the living room," he continues in a hushed tone. "We gathered all the clock bits and packed them into a plastic container. We were in such a hurry that we probably tossed in the photo too. I helped Ev carry the container to her car and expected to go with her, but she wouldn't let me. She said I couldn't keep a secret, and I suppose by telling you this, I've finally proved her right," he adds with a rueful smile. "She never told me where she hid the clock—only that my father wouldn't find it."

"Was he angry that you hid it?" I ask.

"No, because he never knew." Reggie chuckles. "Evaline knocked out a window screen, and I tossed about furniture to make it look like we'd been burgled. No real damage but we made a frightful mess. When Ev let out a bloody scream, I thought my eardrums would burst. My parents came running, and Ev told them we'd interrupted a robbery. I played my role of scared kid very well—no surprise

I ended up as an actor. Dad was devastated to lose his clock, but Mom couldn't stop smiling. And there's never been any more talk of divorce."

"So your sister hid the clock in our shack?" Becca asks.

"Apparently," Reggie answers with a shrug. "I think a friend helped her, probably someone who lived near your sanctuary."

"It wasn't a sanctuary that long ago—just a farmhouse owned by a family with lots of kids," Becca adds. "One of the kids must have known your sister. You could ask her."

"Ev is too tight-lipped to admit anything," Reggie says. "But since you found the clock in your shack and this photo of Granddad, I'm sure that's what happened."

"Our clock mystery is solved," I say excitedly.

"Solved for me too," Reggie says, setting down his mug. "Do you mind if I keep the photo?"

"Of course not." Becca smiles. "It's yours."

"Thank you." He rubs his finger gently over the photo. "I thought I'd never know what happened to the old clock, but now I do. You're quite resourceful kids."

"Leo figured out where you lived." Becca lifts

her hand to Leo for a high five. "Way to go, Leo."

But Leo ignores Becca's raised hand. His shoulders slump as he turns to Reggie. "The clock belongs to you. I guess you'll want it back."

"After all your hard work to fix the old thing?" Reggie shakes his head firmly. "Not a chance. It's yours now."

"But it's a valuable antique and part of your family traditions," Leo points out. "Your father will want it."

"He well might, but Mum would kill him if he tried to get it back." Reggie pats Leo on the shoulder. "I'm all for family traditions. But sometimes a tradition is like playing the same tune over and over. After a while you hate the song so it's time for a new one. I don't want or need the clock. Keep it— but my parents must never find out. I'd rather they stay happily married."

"We won't divulge your secret," Leo says with a widening smile.

Becca stands from the bench. "We shouldn't take any more of your time. Thanks so much for the root beer floats and sharing your story. Come visit anytime at Wild Oaks Sanctuary and you can talk to Mom about volunteering."

"I'd love that." He flashes a pearly grin. "But before you go, there's something I want to show you."

Becca, Leo, and I exchange curious glances, then follow Reggie into his backyard. He courteously opens the gate for us. We enter a spacious yard with a covered patio attached to the house and a large fenced-off area in the back around a sturdy shed. There's an odd smell to the air that reminds of me the bird pond in Wild Oaks Sanctuary.

"This way," Reggie says as he goes to the back gate and unlatches it. "Watch where you step. It could be muddy."

"Do you raise birds?" Becca sniffs and looks around curiously.

"No." He shakes his head, his smile bright with mystery.

The gate bangs behind us as we enter an enclosure with a shallow pond and a muddy island and wild grass. In the center of the island is a large, dark rock.

The "rock" moves and a long, rubbery neck peeks out of a domed shell.

"Meet Albert." Reggie makes a sweeping gesture with his hand. "My granddad's giant Aldabra tortoise."

- Chapter 5 -
Albert

I thought Albert looked big in the photo, but he's even bigger up close.

"He's like a dinosaur." Becca carefully avoids mud puddles as she walks to the edge of the small pond.

"Tortoises and turtles are the longest living reptiles," Leo spouts off. "They've been around for over 250 million years."

Reggie nods. "Many tortoise species are extinct like dinosaurs. But Albert's been in my family for over a century."

"Wow!" Becca exclaims.

I stare in amazement. "Do you know how old he is?"

"Not exactly—about 130 years old. My great-grandmother chose St. Patrick's Day for his birthday, and every year my family throws him a grand birthday party with veggie cake and carrots instead of candles."

"Coolness!" Becca's dark eyes shine. "I love birthday parties."

"Me too." I turn to look at Leo. "What about you?"

Leo shrugs. "Age isn't a cause for celebration. I'm more impressed with this magnificent reptile. Is he friendly?"

Reggie nods. "He loves attention."

Becca and I come over to admire Albert too. He's huge with a really long neck and a bumpy shell that's gray with tan specks.

"May I touch him?" I ask a bit timidly.

"Have a go at it," Reggie says cheerfully.

The armor-like domed shell looks hard as rock and is smooth to touch. Reggie tells us it's called a carapace.

"Hello, Albert," I say as I slide my fingers across his domed shell.

"What gorgeous color patterns," Becca says with a thoughtful expression. "The specks, bumps, and squares would make a beautiful fabric design."

Becca traces her finger over dark patterns on the shell. "Do you mind if I take his picture?"

"Not at all," Reggie says. "Albert is quite an attention seeker. He's been photographed often when people come to see him."

Becca snaps lots of photos, bending close to get Albert's shell at different angles. She designs animal-print fabric for clothes and accessories like the oversized leopard scarf belted around her waist. I predict a tortoise-print outfit in her future.

Albert is friendly and stretches out his neck to be scratched. His wrinkly face reminds me of the alien in that old movie *ET*. And I fall a little in love with him. His dark eyes shine with curiosity as if he understands what we're saying. We pet and talk to Albert until Reggie leads us out of the enclosure.

"I'm going to read up on tortoises when I get home," Leo says excitedly as Reggie locks the gate behind us. "I want to know more about them."

"They have a fascinating history. At the end of the nineteenth century, Charles Darwin worked to save endangered Aldabras by relocating them. Real events can be more exciting than an adventure novel. Do come back to visit Albert—he loves visitors," Reggie says with a welcoming gesture.

"You can come to Wild Oaks," Becca adds. "I'll tell Mom you'll make a fantabulous volunteer. You'd be great at leading tours with your acting skills and cool accent."

"And we can show you the grandfather clock," I say.

Reggie grins. "You'll be hearing from me soon."

We wave good-bye. As I unlock the chain on my bike, I smile at my club mates. "Today has been amazing—and to think it all happened because of a broken clock."

"Not broken anymore," Leo says with a proud lift of his chin.

"I'm inspired after meeting Albert." Becca hops on her bike. "I have all these design ideas buzzing in my head. I'll call them Carapace Chic." She tilts her head toward me. "Want to come over for lunch at my house?"

"Sure," I say with a big grin.

"Not me." Leo shakes his blond head. "I can't go."

"Let me guess why." I roll my eyes. "You're going to the drama storage room to work on some weird techno prop because Frankie can't survive without your help."

"There's nothing weird about a mechanical giraffe leg." Leo completely misses my sarcasm. "Frankie and I have been trying different lubricating oils to stop the leg from creaking. He's worried the noise will distract the actors on stage."

"Is that an oil stain on your vest?" I can't resist teasing because Leo's clothes are usually spotless.

"What stain? Oh." Leo touches a dark spot on his vest, then sniffs. "Yeah, it's oil. I'll have to be more careful."

"Are you part of the drama club now?" Becca asks Leo.

"I'm not interested in drama." He swats the idea away like an annoying insect. "I enjoy assembling mechanical animals. After I finish the giraffe, I'll program the hyena headpieces to raise and lower like they're lunging at each other."

"You can do that?" Becca asks, impressed.

"It's basic robotics." Leo steps on his gyro-board, then turns back to us. "Frankie came up with the idea. He's really smart."

"And sneaky," I remind Leo, my tone sharp with accusation. "Have you forgotten that he followed you to our clubhouse and spied on us?"

"We spy on people too," Leo points out.

"Only when we're trying to help animals," Becca says.

"Frankie followed me because he was curious why I was going into the woods and thought I might need help. He guessed we have a club although I didn't tell him the name or how we help animals. He loves animals too and will want to help out."

"Help out *how*?" I ask with a bad feeling.

"Finding missing pets and solving mysteries." Leo looks at us hopefully. "Can I invite him to join the CCSC?"

"No way!" I shake my head firmly. "I don't trust him."

"He's 100 percent trustworthy," Leo argues.

"We don't need any new members. Tell him, Becca."

Becca looks uneasily back and forth between the two of us. "I've never thought about more members."

"Frankie is already too busy with the drama club." I cross my arms firmly over my chest. "He doesn't have time to look for lost pets or attend club meetings."

Leo taps his chin thoughtfully. "You have a good point, Kelsey."

"I do?" I'm always surprised when Leo agrees with me.

Leo nods. "We need requirements for potential new club members."

"*If* we allow new members," I point out. "I like CCSC with just three of us."

"Three is the perfect number for a club." Becca twists the end of her ponytail. "With four Sparklers we have trouble agreeing on anything."

"But if we do invite someone," I add, trying to be fair, "they'd have to prove they can be trusted, are dedicated to helping animals, and are good at solving puzzling mysteries. Also, it has to be a unanimous vote."

"Unanimous?" Leo frowns at me. "Why not a majority rule?"

"Which majority do you want to rule?" My grip tightens on my handlebars. "What if Becca and I voted in someone you hated?"

"You'd do that?" Leo's blue eyes widen.

"It could happen," I warn.

Leo gulps, then straightens his shoulders. "On second thought, a unanimous vote is an excellent suggestion. Being trustworthy, helping animals, and solving mysteries are good requirements. I'll type up a membership plan, and then we can vote on Frankie at our next meeting."

I nod, although Frankie has a lot of proving to do before he gets *my* vote.

We split up, Leo wheeling off to see Frankie while Becca and I ride our bikes toward her house. We're quiet for a while, pedaling at a slow pace side-by-side.

When we wait at an intersection for little kids to cross the street, Becca smiles at me. "So when does your mother start her new job?"

"Monday." I grin because I'm thrilled about Mom's job as the new animal control officer. The last officer had some honesty issues and moved away. "I can't wait to see her official uniform."

"She'll look amazing." Becca flashes a grin.

"Yeah, I'm happy for her but worried about Dad." I swerve to miss a pothole. "He still can't find a job."

"Ridiculous! A talented chef like him should have employers begging for him. I predict he'll find one soon," Becca says cheerfully. "Then you'll move into a house—hopefully close to me—and take your kitten home."

I cross my fingers and hope, hope, hope. I want

to keep Honey so much. I haven't even told my parents I have a kitten. What's the use? While I live in a no-pets apartment, my kitten stays with Becca.

We coast through downtown Sun Flower, then shift into low gears to pedal up the hill to Wild Oaks Sanctuary. As we ride under the arched entrance, Becca says, "How do sandwiches sound for lunch?"

"Great." My stomach rumbles.

"I make a great BLT."

"Double tomato for me," I say.

"And I'll have a—" Becca's pocket dings. "A text."

"A text for lunch?"

"No, silly, a text on my phone." She stops her bike and takes her phone from her pocket.

"From who?" I brake to a stop beside her.

Becca glances down. "Tyla."

"What does *she* want?" I ask uneasily. I'm trying to like Tyla. Really, I am. But she acts like the Queen of Everyone. And she was the only Sparkler who voted against me temporarily joining the group.

Becca frowns. "Tyla says it's urgent that I come to her house right now."

"Urgent to Tyla can be a broken fingernail," I say.

"Too true." Becca groans. "I really don't want to go."

"So tell her no."

Becca's ponytail slaps her shoulders as she shakes her head. "No one says no to Tyla."

"Start a new trend. Tell her you have better things to do than bow down to her royal commands. It's about time someone stood up to Queen Tyla."

"Maybe—but not me." Her cheeks redden. "It's easier if I just go."

I swallow a big lump of disappointment. "So go."

"You won't mind?"

Of course I mind. But I don't want Becca to feel bad.

When I shake my head, she exhales into a huge smile. "You're the best, Kelsey. Come over tomorrow and we'll do something fun, like eat lunch with the animals."

"Yeah, that'll be great," I say with a forced smile.

We turn around and coast down Wild Road back into downtown Sun Flower. We ride side-by-side until we reach Pleasant Street where we split up. Becca turns left and I pedal on ahead, alone.

I have nothing else to do now except go home.

But as I near the shopping center where my brother biked this morning, I make a detour into the parking lot. I inhale a cheesy aroma from the pizza place and peer around like I'm on a stakeout looking for suspicious activity. Everything seems calm, just random people going in and out of buildings.

What was in Kyle's white box? I think, looking around. *Did he cut through the alley to lose me? Or did he go inside one of the businesses?*

I stare closely at each building.

Even if the café, pawnshop, or lawyer's office were open that early, he wouldn't have gone into them. He'd just eaten breakfast so he wouldn't go to Friendly's Café. He doesn't own anything valuable enough to pawn. And I can't think of any reason he'd consult a lawyer. If Prehistoric Pizza had been open this morning, he would totally have gone there. The TV ads are corny—a costumed dragon flips a giant pizza on his scaly tail and says, "Prehistoric Pizza is historic!" It might not be "historic," but their pizza is delicious.

And now my stomach is growling.

I check my pocket and find a few dollars—enough for one slice.

But I only get halfway across the parking lot before slamming on my brakes. Sheriff Fischer's black-and-white patrol car is parked outside his office. Great! Now I can ask him if he saw my brother. A good spy checks out all clues.

While I'm working up my courage to go into the sheriff's office, Sheriff Fischer steps out of the office. He's not alone. He slips his arm around a dark-haired woman and draws her close to his chest in a very cozy hug.

OMG—it's Becca's mom!

The sheriff and Mrs. Morales are both divorced and went to high school together so they're good friends. I even saw them hold hands once but didn't think it meant anything. Now I'm not so sure.

And when the sheriff kisses her—a big, fat kiss on the lips that lasts a very long time—I almost fall off my bike.

That is not the casual kiss of just a friend. That's the kind of kiss you give someone you're dating. Becca has not said a word about her mom and Sheriff Fischer dating, which can only mean one thing: Becca has no idea.

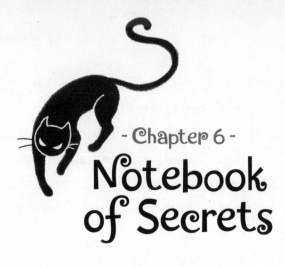

- Chapter 6 -
Notebook of Secrets

When I get home, I race straight into my room and go to my wooden chest. I reach down for the carved decoration on the bottom of the front panel—which is actually a hidden drawer—and take out my notebook of secrets.

I can't stop thinking about the Kiss. When Becca told me her mother was having brunch with a friend, I'm sure she didn't know the friend was the sheriff, or that they were doing more than having brunch. Becca once confided to me that she expects her mother and father to get back together someday.

Wrong, I think as I sink onto my bed.

Becca will be crushed when I tell her...if I tell her.

First this secret is going down on paper with the others I collected today.

Usually secrets come slowly, like waiting for weekends or birthdays. If I uncover one a month, that's more than the average. Yet today I learned *four* secrets. And they're not little ones either, like when my sisters snuck out to an over-eighteen club or my father used a butter substitute in his famous sugar crumb cookies.

All four are *big* secrets. And two of them are about my club mates.

Sitting at my desk with a pen and notebook, I think back to this morning when I followed Kyle on my bike.

Secret 32. Reserved for the secret "something" in Kyle's white box.

Secret 33. Leo is only eleven years old and will turn twelve soon. His mother is planning a surprise birthday party.

Secret 34. Reggie and his sister faked a robbery to get rid of the grandfather clock.

Secret 35. The sheriff and Becca's mom
kissed!

Writing down the secrets helps me see them clearer. Although I was shocked at first to find out Leo's age, now that it's sunken in, it isn't a big deal. So what if he's younger than me? He's still my friend.

And it was cool listening to Reggie's story, then meeting Albert. A 130-year-old tortoise—wow! Albert is more than *twelve* times my age.

But the last secret is different. I rub my chin as I reread Secret 35: The sheriff and Becca's mom kissed. Mrs. Morales and the sheriff are both single, so why shouldn't they date? Maybe he's crushed on her since high school and ignored their feelings until she was divorced. Really, it's sweet and romantic.

Unfortunately, Becca won't see it that way.

When she finds out, will she be shocked or angry, or burst into tears?

Secrets are dangerous; they can destroy lives. If revealed, Reggie's could damage his parents' marriage. If other kids find out Leo is only eleven, they'll tease him (even more than some do now). But Becca deserves to know about her mother.

How can I balance truth and lies to protect my friends?

Thinking so hard makes my head hurt. I lean back on a pillow, feeling exhausted. Yawning, I close my eyes and sink into sleep.

Footsteps. A knock on my door.

My eyes pop open and I look over at the clock. Drats! I've slept over two hours!

"Kelsey, are you in there?" my mom calls out softly.

"Yes, Mom. Just a sec," I say when I spot my notebook of secrets sitting out in plain sight on my bed. Quickly, I grab it and return it to the hidden drawer. Just in time too, because Mom peeks into my room.

"Just letting you know that dinner's ready," she says.

"Dinner already?" I repeat, realizing I missed lunch. "Okay. I'm coming." I jump up and follow her out of my room.

It's a family rule to eat dinner together at the dining table, and I'm last to arrive. As I chew homemade sourdough bread, my gaze settles on Kyle. I study my brother like a speck of blood under a CSI microscope, trying to guess where he went this morning and what was hidden in his box. Where could he have disappeared to right in front of my eyes? I keep hoping he'll bring up the topic, but all he talks about (as usual) are strategies for getting a full-ride scholarship.

When he asks me to pass the bread, I hand him the basket and ask casually, "So how did the heavy lifting go today?"

"Huh?" Kyle's face goes blank like someone clicked Delete in his brain.

I smile sweetly, amused that he doesn't remember the excuse he gave when he rode off on his bike this morning. "With your old buddy Jake?"

"Oh yeah, Jake." He blinks fast. "Everything was cool."

I almost laugh because if he really did lift heavy furniture today, he'd complain about sore muscles. Kyle is so bad at lying. My brother is definitely up to something—and soon the CCSC will be on the case.

Later that night, I reach up to my bookshelf and take down my favorite book. Curling up against my pillows, I flip the book open to Chapter One of

Harriet the Spy. Whenever I have more questions than answers, I turn to Harriet for advice.

Skimming pages, I pause at the scene where Harriet's friend Sport asks to go spying with her. Harriet replies, "Spies don't go with friends."

My eyes grow heavy and the book falls from my fingers. I think of my spying adventures with the CCSC: going on stakeouts, solving mysteries, and reuniting lost pets with their owners.

Harriet got it wrong, I think as I drift off to sleep. Spying is better with friends.

- Chapter 7 -

Fit-Pic

The next day nothing goes as planned.

While I'm chewing Dad's corn-flake-crusted French toast, Becca calls the house phone.

"Hey, Kelsey," she says but without her usual cheerfulness.

I swallow and ask, "Is something up?"

"How'd you know?" She sighs. "I can't make lunch today."

"Are you sick?"

"Sick of Tyla," she gripes. "Remember that urgent problem she had yesterday? Well, her bratty brother threw her cosmetic case with all the face paints into their pool."

"I bet the pool looked like someone vomited in

it," I joke.

Instead of laughing, Becca groans. "The Sparklers needed those paints for our fund-raiser booth."

"Wait a minute." My brain whirls. "They decided on a face-painting booth instead of one of the cool ideas we suggested?"

"Tyla hated all our ideas. Since her face paints are destroyed, new ones have to be bought. And Tyla insists that I go with her."

"Can't Tyla shop by herself?" I glare at the phone.

"Yeah—if shopping were an Olympic sport, she'd win gold medals. But I'm the Sparkler treasurer so she wants me to go with her. I dread it because before we buy paints, she'll drag me into every store and make me wait while she tries on clothes."

"Sounds fun. Not."

"It won't be as torturous if you're there." Becca's voice rises with hope. "Please, please, come with us."

An afternoon with the Queen of Everything criticizing what I wear, say, and do? No, thank you.

When I return to eating my breakfast, my French toast is soggy and cold, like how I feel inside.

Before I have time for a pity party, the phone rings again.

For a hopeful moment I think Becca is calling back to say we can hang out today. But it's my grandmother with an invitation to my family—a Fitness Picnic in the park.

I start smiling. We hadn't had a Fit-Pic in months. Gran Nola, a yoga instructor, organizes a game of exercises with prizes for most graceful, highest achievement, and fastest. And if there's a race, our dog Handsome runs with us.

Mom says this is just what she needs to avoid thinking about "pre-first-day-on-the-job jitters," and Dad can't wait to get started on the menu for the Fit-Pic. He consults with my grandmother on the phone, rattling off food choices, and then rushes to the kitchen to get ready. I expect my brother to stay home to study or my sisters to hurry off to be with friends. But they actually seem excited to hang out as a family—something we rarely do since moving to the apartment.

We find the perfect picnic table in a ring of shady oaks. And while Dad sets out a feast, Mom joins us kids for Gran Nola's fitness games.

"Our first contest is the William Tell," Gran announces and then passes out apples.

We place apples on our heads and twist into whatever yoga pose Gran shouts out. Whoever poses longest without dropping their apple wins (and Gran always comes prepared with wrapped prizes). The Cobbler's Pose and Cow Face Pose are easy. Difficulty increases with the Eagle Pose. Mom loses her balance and laughs as she—and her apple—fall to the grass. The King Dancer Pose takes out both Kyle and Kiana, leaving me and Kenya. So it's a pose-off! We balance on one foot with our other leg bent and our palms praying. I'm doing good, my focus steady, until my nose itches and I sneeze. Kenya whoops over her win.

Gran Nola announces the fitness race, and all the kids line up.

This isn't a run-to-the-finish-line race. Nothing is that simple with Gran Nola. She sets up three fitness challenges: hula-hoop, jump rope, and headstand. Mom and Dad are judges as we complete each task. My sisters are great at hula-hooping and finish at the same time. Not so easy for me. The hula-hoop circles more often around my ankles than my waist. But I finally achieve the fifty spins needed to go on to jump roping. I'm quick at jump roping and make up time. At the finish though, it's my brother who wins by standing on his head for five minutes.

"Guess your big head is good for something," Kenya teases.

We all laugh, then sit down for a picnic that should go down in history as the Best. Lunch. Ever. Dad even prepared special canine cuisine for Handsome.

While I'm chomping on a happy face cupcake, Handsome barks and then pokes his Frisbee at my leg.

"Want to play?" I ask, then swallow the last bite of cupcake.

Handsome barks excitedly, his dark eyes shining. There are too many trees around our picnic table, so I lead him to a grassy area and throw the Frisbee. After several throws, I notice another dog—a Queensland healer—watching us.

The dog is about twenty feet away, half-hidden in the shade of a green bush. The medium-sized healer has short, gray-brown fur and a cropped tail. There's a longing look on his face, as if he wants to play Frisbee too. I glance around for his owner but don't see anyone.

And that's when my brain clicks.

I've seen this dog before—or at least his photo on a lost pet flyer. I'm sure it's the same dog, and he's been missing for over a week.

Slowly, I stand up and hold out the Frisbee.

"Hey, boy," I say softly. "Want to play with us?"

The dog looks up at me but doesn't move. But Handsome barks and lunges for the Frisbee. "Sit, Handsome," I whisper. "Stay."

Handsome whines a complaint, but he's well trained and sits. His gaze stays on the new dog though, playful and friendly.

I take a careful step forward, holding out the Frisbee like I'm offering a yummy dog treat. "Come over here and you can play with us."

The healer's stubby tail wags, and I can read eagerness in his blue eyes. But there's fear too. He backs away.

"I won't hurt you," I promise sweetly. "Come here and get the Frisbee. I have dog treats back at our table. You'll be safe with me."

The dog hangs its head and whines.

"It's okay, boy," I say soothingly. "I'll take you back to your owner. Come here and everything will be fine."

That stubby tail wiggles, and I think he's starting to trust me.

I take another step, then another and—the blur of gray-brown fur spins around and vanishes into the bushes.

"Come back!" I call, running around the bushes. But there's no sign of him.

Drats. I lift up the Frisbee and resume playing with Handsome. But I keep an eye out for the Queensland healer. Unfortunately, he never returns.

Later that night, I search through missing pets flyers until I find a photo of the Queensland healer. His name is Bobbsey. He's ten months old and loves to run and jump—which is how he escaped from his yard. His owner is offering a twenty-five-dollar reward.

I'll show this flyer to Becca and Leo when we meet at the Skunk Shack tomorrow. Then we'll bike around looking for lost pets, which is always fun. It might be awkward though, because I won't be able to look at Leo and Becca without thinking of the secrets I uncovered.

Sighing, I take my notebook of secrets out of the hidden drawer. I curl up against my pillows and read through the latest entries. I imagine how each person would feel if I exposed their secrets, which reminds me how important it is to write down secrets instead of talking about them.

With a yawn, I close my notebook. I'm so tired I could sleep for a week. I reach for my pajamas, then stop when I glance at my backpack. Drats! I almost forgot my algebra homework. (Why teachers assign homework over the weekend is a mystery to me!)

I take out my textbook and paper but can't find a pencil. I turn my backpack upside down, dumping its contents onto my bed. Finally, a pencil! I lean back against pillows and get to work. When the last algebra equation is done, I toss everything into my backpack, then turn off the light.

Sunlight stabs my eyes.

Morning already?

I glance at the clock. Already half past seven? I'm running late!

Usually Mom wakes me when I oversleep, but her new work hours are even earlier than my school hours. And Dad is busy making breakfast.

I stagger out of bed, my muscles a little sore from

yoga poses. I move slowly like a tortoise when I need to be speedy like a rabbit.

After I get dressed, I tame my tangled hair into a ponytail and brush my teeth. As I'm leaving the bathroom, there's a *thud* from my brother's room. Kyle rushes out of his room, carrying toiletries and a change of clothes. He brushes past me on his way to shower, mutters "sorry," and then slams the bathroom door.

Immediately, I jump into action.

This is my chance to search his room.

- Chapter 8 -
What I Found

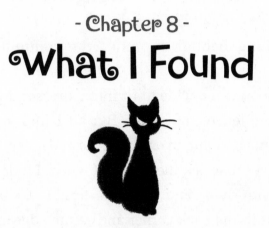

My sisters treat showering like a vacation destina-
tion—packing luggage and moving into the bathroom
for an hour or two. But not Kyle. He never takes
more than ten minutes. Will that be enough time?

With a furtive glance down the hall, I duck into
Kyle's room. I leave the door open a crack so I can
hear the rush of running water. As soon as the
shower stops, I'm out of here.

My brother's room isn't much bigger than
mine, but it feels spacious because he's so neat.
Everything has an orderly place; his desk is spotless
with supplies such as pens and paper organized on
shelves. His bedspread doesn't have any wrinkles.
And no socks or shoes clutter the floor.

Where would he hide a large box? I tap my chin and slowly turn in a circle to gaze around the room.

Nothing under the bed.

Nothing behind or under the computer desk either.

The box is too wide to fit into a dresser drawer so that only leaves the closet. But all I find are shirts and pants hanging in order of size and color. I drag a chair over to check the top shelf where I hide my spy pack in my own room. No luck—until I look behind a suitcase in the back corner and see an edge of white.

The mysterious box!

My heart pounds as I shove the suitcase aside. I have to move quickly. The box is bigger than I realized; about three feet long and six inches deep. But it's surprisingly light, like holding a balloon.

And when I lift off the lid...

Nothing.

Why would Kyle hide an empty box? Something important must have been inside it—but what? And how will I ever find out?

I start to put the lid back on when sunbeams from the bedroom window behind me shine on a tiny green spot inside the box.

Only it's not a spot.

I pick up a flat, round piece of plastic. It's olive-green, the size of a quarter but thinner and bendy. Both sides are smooth with no identifying marks.

What is this? And why hide a tiny green circle in a large box?

Before I can come up with any ideas, I realize it's quiet.

The rush of shower water has stopped. As soon as Kyle dries off, he'll come in here to get ready for school.

Drats. I have to get out of here!

I shove the box back behind the suitcase. I don't realize I'm still holding the green circle (a gaming disk, maybe?) until I'm already back in my room. The bathroom door creaks open, and Kyle's bare feet shuffle against the worn hallway carpet.

Whew!

Sinking into my computer chair, I turn the coin-sized plastic disk over in my palm. *What are you?*

No time to figure it out now.

When I hear Dad calling my name from downstairs, I slip the disk into my pocket and grab my backpack. I race to the kitchen and slather a bagel with strawberry cream cheese. I'm halfway out the door when Dad taps my shoulder.

"Don't forget this." He grins as he hands me a sack lunch.

"Thanks!" I kiss his cheek, then hurry out of the apartment. I take two stairs at a time to the bike rack where I unlock my bike and pedal so fast I make it to school as the warning bell rings.

I usually stop by my locker, but instead I go straight to my homeroom. The bell rings as I slump into my desk.

"Made it!" I whisper in exhausted relief.

Becca turns around from her desk and gives me a thumbs-up.

When my teacher, Ms. Grande, isn't watching, Becca and I exchange notes.

I looked n K box! I write to her.

She replies, ?????!!!!!

Show U @ break.

Now, she insists.

Leaning forward, I stretch my arm out beneath my desk and open my palm. Green plastic shines.

Becca's brows knit with questions. But I shrug and mouth, "Later." My teacher must have psychic hearing because she calls my name and wags a warning finger at me. So we wait to talk until between classes when we meet at my locker.

"What is this?" Becca picks up the plastic circle, twirling it in her fingers while kids swarm past us in the hall.

"No idea," I say. "I hoped you'd know."

"It could be a sequin or button except no holes."

"Jewelry?" I guess.

"Not very good jewelry if it is." Becca's glittery hair clip sparkles as she shakes her head. "It might be a game piece."

"I wondered about that too, but Kyle isn't a gamer," I say firmly. "He's more into sports—at least he was before he got so obsessed with applying for scholarships and studying his SAT prep book."

"You don't know what's he's involved with now," Becca points out.

"He *has* been acting really suspicious." I spin my locker combination and open the door. "I'm positive he knew I was following him when he biked off with the white box, and he lost me by cutting through the mini mall."

"Or he went into the sheriff's office," Becca says. "I think you should talk to Sheriff Fischer."

"No." I think of the Kiss and hide my reddening face as I take my science textbook from my backpack and place it in my locker.

"Why not?"

"I don't want to bother the sheriff." I bite my lip.

"Sheriff Fischer won't mind," Becca persists. "He's known Mom since they were kids, and when he comes over, he's super nice, not like a sheriff but more like an uncle."

Or a future stepdad, I think.

"He's easy to talk to," Becca adds. "If you won't talk to him, I will."

"No! Don't!" I snap, then see Becca's surprised expression and soften my voice. "I mean, I'm positive Kyle didn't go there. My brother may be acting sneaky, but he'd never get involved in anything illegal."

"You can never be...OMG!" Her eyes go wide and she gasps. "Is that what I think it is?"

"What?" I look around but don't see anything shock-worthy.

"In your backpack." Becca points. "I can't believe you brought it to school."

I follow her gaze, and my stomach lurches like I've tumbled into a black hole. My backpack hangs open off my shoulder so some stuff is visible—including an ordinary-looking notebook that is far from ordinary.

How did my notebook of secrets get into my backpack?

- Chapter 9 -
Secret's Out

I think back to when I last saw my notebook. I was writing in it on my bed, and then I did homework. I couldn't find a pencil and dumped stuff out of my backpack until I finally found one. I finished my homework late and was so tired I could hardly keep my eyes open. When I tossed everything back into my backpack, I must have included the notebook.

"So it *is* that notebook!" Becca's eyes pop wide.

"Shhh!" I put my finger to my lips and glance around the hall. No one is in sight, but that doesn't stop my heart from thundering like a perfect storm.

"It's just a plain notebook," she says, sounding disappointed. "I expected something glittery with a dramatic cover."

"Keep your voice down." I glance around nervously.

Becca swivels her head to look up, then down the hall. "No one's around to hear what we say."

"And we should go too. I don't want to be tardy."

"But I want to see your notebook. We still have a few minutes before the final bell," she whispers. "Didn't you bring it to show me?"

"I didn't even know it was in my backpack." I hang my head in misery. "It was a horrible mistake."

Her smile fades. "I really want to read it. I've been curious about your notebook since you told me you collected secrets."

"But I never show anyone."

"Not even those sporty girls from your old neighborhood?"

"No." I drop my voice to a whisper. "I wrote secrets about Ann Marie and Tori too."

"Did they cheat in a game or blackmail a referee? I swear I won't tell anyone." Becca's gaze sweeps longingly over my notebook.

I shake my head. "A secret wouldn't be a secret if I told."

"But I already know some of them." Her black, purple-streaked ponytail sways as she bobs her head. "You wrote about Reggie's grandfather clock, didn't you?"

"Well, yeah."

"And you already told me about hiding so well that your parents reported you missing and you pretended you'd been kidnapped."

"Don't talk about that!" I put my finger to my lips. "My parents would freak if they knew the truth."

"You were only five." Becca rolls her dark eyes. "Besides, they must have guessed what really happened or they'd never let you go anywhere. Parents are smart."

"Still, I don't want anyone to know." I push the notebook deep inside my backpack. "I only told you because, well, we're friends and this secret was about me. But other secrets I write down aren't mine to share. Sorry, I can't show you my notebook."

"I won't tell anyone." Becca lowers her voice. "I can't help being curious. You'd feel the same way."

"You know me too well," I admit with a wry smile.

"And you know me enough to know you can trust me."

She's right—and I'm so tempted to show her my notebook. Some of the secrets would shock her;

others would make her laugh; and a few might make her cry. But if I can't trust myself to keep a secret, how can I trust anyone else? I feel like a superhero on a sacred mission to protect my notebook: *Kelsey Case, Guardian of Secrets.*

But there is one secret I should tell her...

"I found out something yesterday about your mo—" I'm interrupted by the school bell. "Tell you at lunch. Meet me outside the cafeteria, by the rosebushes."

"Oh, I'll be there!" Becca jumps. "I can't wait!"

I can, I think uneasily as we leave the locker.

During my next classes, I stare out the windows and mentally rehearse how to tell Becca that her parents won't be getting back together. But bad news still sounds like bad news, no matter how you rearrange the words.

When the lunch bell rings, I head for the cafeteria. I don't hurry, uneasy about spilling a secret to Becca. Everyone I see makes me think of secrets. I pass a girl in the hall, Samantha Keystone, and remember her secret: she lives outside the school district so she pretends to live with her grandmother. An eighth-grade guy playing in the hoop court, Erik Taylor, anonymously posts cartoons as the Corning Comic, mocking kids at school. I keep walking, past hordes of noisy kids flooding through cafeteria doors, and wave at Mr. Thompson, the groundskeeper (a secret reality-show winner), as he clips a hedge.

Finally I spot Becca's leopard-print blouse through the thorny branches of a rosebush.

She's bouncing from foot to foot, excited because she has no idea what I'm going to tell her. She thinks secrets are fun—like when Reggie told us about the grandfather clock. But this secret won't make her smile.

"So, spill!" Becca clasps my arm. "What's the secret?"

"Not here where people can see us." I lead her around to the side of the cafeteria. The dumpster is nearby, and the air smells of dead, decaying things.

"Secrets aren't a matter of life or death," Becca teases.

"They can be." I shift my heavy backpack to the other shoulder.

She laughs like she thinks I'm joking.

Now is the time to spill what I know...but first, some procrastination.

"Did I ever tell you why I started collecting secrets?" I ask.

"No. I thought it was something you've always done."

"I started my notebook in fifth grade," I explain. "Before that I was just a snoopy kid. But that changed the night I went to a friend's slumber party."

"What happened?" Becca leans in closer.

"I woke up thirsty so I went to the kitchen for some water. I was putting my glass in the sink when I heard my friend's parents arguing in the living room. I found out they were getting a divorce and were waiting to tell their kids after a few fun days at Disneyland. I was shocked and ran back to the bedroom. I was going to tell my friend—only I couldn't."

"Why not? She would have wanted to know," Becca says with such certainty that I know she's thinking of her own divorced parents.

"Her parents had to tell her—not me." I shake my head. "It was hard to keep such a big secret to myself. So I wrote it down in a notebook, which made me feel better, like I was telling someone even if it was only me. After that, secrets seemed to find me—or sometimes I'd find them." I flash a wicked grin. "Lip-reading is a useful tool for the curious."

"You're the most curious person I know," Becca says.

"Except you." I smile.

"And Leo." She lifts her hand, curving her fingers into a *C*. We knuckle-tap the CCSC secret hand bump and finish by air-shaping the letter *S*.

"But secrets can hurt people," I add seriously. "I found out the hard way."

Becca's eyes go wide. "What happened?"

"My aunt Missy was visiting from Oregon. I overheard Dad teasing Mom that her sister had dead-fish breath, and he called her 'Fishy Missy.' I thought it was funny so I told my aunt what Dad called her."

"Ouch."

"Major ouch," I say. "I thought my aunt would think it was funny too—but she started crying. She ran out of the room and packed her bags, then left, and wouldn't talk to my parents for a year. Telling what I overheard hurt my whole family. After that, I hid my secrets in my notebook and never showed anyone. Sorry, not even you."

"I understand." Becca twists her ponytail. "Keep your notebook in your backpack. I don't want to see it."

"But I said I'd tell you a secret."

"Is it about me?" she asks with raised brows.

"No...someone...um...you know really well."

"Stop right there." She gives a sassy snap of her fingers. "I don't want to know. I'd try to keep it a secret, but what if it accidentally slipped out the way you did with your aunt? I don't want to hurt anyone's feelings—even if it's by mistake." Becca puts her hands over her ears. "Do. Not. Tell. Me."

So I don't, and I'm relieved. Her mother will tell her when she's ready.

Becca and I join the mass of kids in the cafeteria, slipping back into routine. She waits in line for her food, while I take my sack lunch to the Sparkler table. It still feels weird to wear a Sparkler necklace and sit with the school glitterati. It's fun but I'm glad it's only temporary. I'm not the glittery type and am more comfortable sitting with friends from my old neighborhood, Ann Marie and Tori.

As I wait for the Sparklers to get their hot lunches, I glance over at the next table where Ann Marie and Tori loudly debate a track meet. I'm not sports-obsessed like them, but we get along great because we've known each other since kindergarten. Our parents called us the "Turbo Triplets" since we did everything together until I moved into an apartment on the other side of town.

My gaze shifts to the back of the room where Leo always eats alone.

But wait a minute! Solitary Leo, who prefers to design robots on his electronic tablet rather than socialize, is *not* alone.

Frankie sits beside him, his lanky shoulders bent over so his green cap covers his face.

"What are you staring at?" Becca asks, slipping into the seat beside me.

"Not what—*who*." I point and she draws in a sharp breath.

"Leo is talking to another human instead of his electronic tablet," Becca says in disbelief. "The world must be ending."

"Or we've slipped into a parallel universe."

"But it's a nice universe because Leo looks happy. I'm glad he has another friend. He's breaking out of his shell and getting more social."

I nod, realizing Leo's awkwardness with other kids isn't just because he's so smart. Knowing his real age explains a lot.

"Frankie is cool," Becca adds. "He works hard for the drama club and doesn't seem to care what anyone thinks of him. You may not like Frankie but Leo does, and that's good enough for me. I think we should vote Frankie into the CCSC."

"I don't dislike Frankie—it's all about trust. He lied to us when we were searching for the zorse's mask. He has to prove he's trustworthy."

"And how is he supposed to do that if you don't give him a chance?" Becca frowns like I'm being unreasonable.

I can't think of an answer and am relieved to drop the subject when the Sparklers—Chloe, Sophia, and Tyla—join us.

Chloe sits across from me, blue-haired with big, jeweled glasses and an even bigger personality. She's the leader of the Sparklers. Spiked-hair Sophia slips beside her. Even though Sophia has a starring role in the drama club's *Lion King*, she's surprisingly shy. Last to arrive is tall, brown-eyed Tyla. She sits on the other side of Becca and ignores me as usual, as if pretending I'm not there will make it true.

"Wait till you see the new face paints—neon with glitter!" Tyla plops down a tray of hot food and turns to the other girls. "And Becca came up with some cute face-art designs, not the usual fairies and rainbows, but mythological creatures and anime characters."

"Drawing comes easy to me," Becca says with a modest shrug. "But the paints cost more than I expected. We shouldn't have bought so many."

"Not to worry, Madame Treasurer." Tyla cuts her off with an air swish of her hand. "We'll charge more and make so much money the other booths will be jealous." She launches into details about her face-painting plans and I tune her out. We get along best when we ignore each other.

Opening my brown bag, I take out my lunch. I feel sorry for kids who suffer through boring cafeteria food while I have my own personal chef. Chef Dad doesn't just *make* lunch; he creates culinary art. Carved carrot sticks, salads with smiling tomato cherry faces, and themed sandwiches. Today's sandwich is sesame-seed bread with raspberry jelly, cream cheese, and cucumber slices. And my mouth is already watering for the homemade cookies.

When the Sparklers first tasted Dad's cookies, they oohed like they'd gone to cookie heaven. Now Dad packs extras for them.

I take caramel shortbread cookies out of my bag

and conversation stops. Eager hands reach out, and abracadabra! Cookies disappear.

Ah, the magic of Dad's baking.

"Best cookie ever." Chloe always says this.

"Deliciousness!" Becca smacks her lips.

Sophia gives me a thumbs-up.

And even Tyla murmurs, "Yum."

But the spell ends too soon, and Tyla turns back into a snarky queen.

"I'll be in charge of our booth at the fund-raiser," she says. "Becca will assist me in face painting. The rest of you will decorate the booth, collect money, wash paintbrushes, and clean up."

Chloe taps her finger to her chin. "I have relatives visiting and can't get there until noon."

"I'll help in the morning." Sophia raises her hand like she's in a classroom. "But I have to leave before two for play rehearsals."

Tyla throws up her hands. "You expect me to do everything?"

"Kelsey and I will be there," Becca points out.

"Like she'll be much help now that we've decided on a booth idea," Tyla says with a scowl at me. "I bought the paints and will do most of the face painting. What are you going to contribute?"

I'd rather quit than answer her, but I'm not a quitter.

"I'll stay at the booth all day," I say through gritted teeth.

"And do what?" Tyla presses her lips together.

"Greet customers, take money, and clean up."

Tyla shrugs. "Anyone can do that."

"I was *asked* to be a temporary Sparkler," I retort. "If you don't want my help, you can—"

"But we do want your help, Kelsey, and I'm really glad you're here," Becca says in a gentle tone like a crisis mediator. "I'll make a booth schedule." She glances around the table. "Anyone got a pen and paper?"

"Use mine." I unzip my backpack and push papers aside, feeling for my favorite pink pen.

"Kelsey, give her a piece of paper too," Tyla says, pointing.

"What paper?" I don't know what she's talking about until she swoops down for my backpack.

Tyla grabs my notebook of secrets.

- Chapter 10 -
Keep Away

"*No!*" I shout and lunge for my notebook.

"Get over yourself already, Kelsey." Tyla steps back with an exaggerated roll of her glitter-shadowed eyes. "Losing one sheet of paper from your notebook isn't going to kill you."

Oh, I am so dead.

I make another grab for my book, but Tyla jerks it away. Dangly star earrings jangle as she tilts her head toward me. "Why are you freaking out over a dumb notebook?"

"I'm not!"

"I don't believe you." She reads the cover, then laughs. "Notebook of secrets?"

"That's private!" I growl like a lion protecting

her cub and make another grab for my notebook.

But Tyla moves back, staring curiously at me. "As if any secret of yours could interest me."

"You're right. I'm boring," I say. "My notebook is boring too, so return it."

"I will—when I'm ready."

"It's mine." I try to sound dangerous, but my fingers shake as I hold out my hand. "I gave Becca a pen so someone else can give her a piece of paper."

"Actually I have my own paper." Becca rips paper from a binder and slaps it on the table. "I don't need any from Kelsey so return the note-book, Tyla."

"Not until I read a few pages," Tyla says with a gleam in her dark eyes.

"No!" I lunge for her but she steps up on her chair, waving the notebook high over her head like it's a game of keep-away.

Safely out of my reach, Tyla flips through the pages. "So much writing—almost every page is filled! Are you writing a book?'

"Give it back," I say with a desperate look at Becca for help.

But Becca glances uneasily back and forth between Tyla and me, saying nothing.

I ball my fists to show I'm serious. "Hand me the notebook, or I'll — "

"You'll what?" Tyla laughs. "I'm faster and taller than you, so you can't get it from me until I decide to give it to you. You're only a temporary Sparkler, so you may not understand that in a close group like ours, keeping secrets is rude."

"So is stealing someone else's private property," I say.

"Borrowing," she corrects. "Here's a personality tip — if you act selfish, people won't like you."

"I am *not* selfish! I bring extra desserts to lunch and share them with you. All you ever share is a bad attitude!" I glare at Tyla, hatred running lava hot through my body. "My notebook is personal. Return it *now*."

"Why should I?" Tyla dodges when I grab for the book.

"Because it's mine! Give. It. Back." My voice echoes around the room and the cafeteria quiets, heads turning toward us.

"Not before I find out what's inside. What are you hiding?" She flips it open and starts reading, "Secret 1 — "

"*Stop!*" I shout. "Do not say another word! No

one can read it."

"Oh, really?" Tyla arches her brows. "Not even Becca? You're spending so much time with her that I assumed you'd tell her everything." She turns to Becca, whose face blushes bright red. "Have you read it?"

Becca shakes her head no.

"Doesn't that make you wonder what she's hiding?" Tyla points at me.

"Um…no." Becca squirms uneasily between us.

"You have no idea what's in here?" Tyla dramatically waves my notebook in the air. "What if she wrote mean stuff about you?"

I expect Becca to defend me, but she's looking down at her tray, stirring her fork in mushy mashed potatoes.

"She can't have enough secrets of her own to fill so many pages. I bet she wrote about all of us." Tyla turns to each of the Sparklers, her words slithering suspicion around the table.

Chloe, who has always been friendly to me, narrows her eyes. "Kelsey, did you write about me?"

Only one secret, I think. *And it's not that embarrassing.*

"Look at her guilty expression!" Tyla pounces.

"I'm so right about her. She wrote secrets about us."

"Not me," Chloe says confidently. "I don't have any secrets."

But she does, I think. *They all do.*

In the short time I've been around the Sparklers, I've learned more than they realize by listening and lip-reading.

Spy strategy 14: When the truth won't work, create a believable lie.

"Tyla, I'm flattered you think my notebook is so interesting," I say calmly and even manage a faint smile. "But it's not. I just wrote down my weird dreams. Haven't you ever heard of dream journaling?"

"This says 'secrets,' not 'dreams,'" she argues.

"The secrets are only about my dreams."

"Like I believe that," she snorts, still holding my notebook out of reach.

"Honestly." I cross my heart with one hand and cross my fingers behind my back with the other.

"*Liar!*" Tyla accuses so loudly that now everyone in the cafeteria, even the lunch workers, stare at us. "You wrote lies about all of us."

"I didn't!" I argue. *Everything I wrote is true.*

"Easy to prove," Tyla says smugly, then opens my notebook.

Panic hurts worse than a punch to my gut. My notebook is like Pandora's box. If the secrets are released into the world, the knowledge will cause chaos. But Tyla is holding the book tightly as the other Sparklers, even Becca, lean closer to listen.

"Secret 1," Tyla says loud enough for everyone in the cafeteria to hear. "*I wore my Scooby-Doo pajamas to my first sleepover.*" She giggles. "Not much of a secret, just pathetic fashion sense. Oh, but there's more!"

"Please stop." I'm begging now.

"But this is so much fun." Tyla dodges my grab again, then continues. "*It was after midnight and I woke up thirsty, so I went into the kitchen for a glass of water. That's when I overheard—*"

"Stop right there!" a sharp voice interrupts. "Give the notebook to Kelsey."

A hand touches my shoulder, and I turn around to find Tori and Ann Marie standing protectively behind me. When we were young, our Turbo Trio always defended each other. Back then, we were scrawny and usually ended up scraped and bruised. Now my athletic friends are tall and fierce.

"Go back to the other jocks," Tyla says with a dismissive hand flip.

"Kelsey is our friend," Ann Marie says. "Mess with her and you have to mess with us."

"Seriously? You're threatening me?" Tyla glares. "Butt out. This doesn't involve you."

"It will if you don't return Kelsey's notebook," Ann Marie warns. "*Now.*"

"No one tells me what to do," Tyla scoffs. "I don't even know you."

"And you don't want to." When Tori puts her hands on her hips and juts out her chin, she seems even taller and tougher. "We don't like you upsetting our friend."

"Kelsey's an honorary Sparkler and one of my closest friends," Tyla says in such a phony voice I want to vomit. "Can't you see we were just joking around?"

"Kelsey isn't laughing." Ann Marie's scowl deepens.

"Some people need to grow a sense of humor." Tyla rolls her eyes. "I wasn't really going to read her notebook."

Ann Marie glares. "So you won't mind giving it back."

"Sure, sure." Tyla flings the notebook at me.

I hug it to my chest and turn to Ann Marie and Tori. "Thanks."

Ann Marie leans close to whisper in my ear. "Dump these glitter clones and sit with us."

I glance at Becca, hurt that she didn't defend me. I don't want to stay where I'm not welcome. But if I leave, I may never come back—the ultimate win for Tyla. I shake my head at Ann Marie. "I'm okay here."

"Really?" Tori scowls at the Sparklers.

"It's just temporary." I touch the borrowed crescent moon necklace I'm wearing. "I'm only here to help out with the fund-raiser. Next week I'll go back to sitting at our table."

I watch Becca, hoping she'll say I don't have to be "temporary," that I can sit with the Sparklers whenever I want. But she's looking down at her lunch tray as if cafeteria food is fascinating.

Ann Marie pats my shoulder. "Stop by my house soon. It's been too long since you've been over. Mom was asking what's up with you."

"I will," I promise as I zip my notebook securely in my backpack.

After Tori and Ann Marie leave, there's an

awkward silence at our table. Sparklers chew and sip drinks, their gazes sliding away from me as if I've turned into Medusa and one look will turn them into stone.

Finally Becca looks up from her tray and gives a nervous laugh.

"Oookay. Let's get back to fund-raiser business." She taps her pencil against her food tray and looks around the table. "I'll start by making the booth schedule."

Conversation resumes like everything is fine, and the cafeteria noisily buzzes back to life too. But something has changed...me, I think. I'm an outsider among strangers. When lunch ends, I hurry away without saying good-bye to Becca.

To avoid a repeat of the notebook keep-away game, I lock my notebook securely inside my locker, burying it beneath books and a sweater, then slam the locker shut.

I'm still shaking like I'm suffering from PTSD: post-Tyla stress disorder. I can't concentrate in my classes and mentally replay the lunchroom drama.

My old friends stuck up for me, not my new ones. Not Becca.

Why didn't she try to help me? Does Tyla intimidate her *that* much? Or is she more loyal to the other girls than to me? She said I could trust her with my secrets—but can I trust her with my friendship?

When my last class ends, Becca is waiting for me outside the door.

Anger and hurt steam inside me. I can't pretend that everything is okay.

But before I can speak, Becca says, "I'm really, really, really sorry."

"You should be," I say as I walk away from her.

"Let me explain." She follows, hurrying beside me. "Please don't be mad."

"Friends stick up for each other. You did nothing." My backpack bounces on my back as I walk faster. "But it doesn't matter now because Ann Marie and Tori helped."

"It matters," Becca says miserably. "I hate myself for wimping out, and you probably hate me too."

"No, I don't." I stop in the middle of the hall, kids moving around us, and lower my voice. "But why didn't you stick up for me?"

"I tried to." Her lower lip trembles. "When I got

my own paper, I thought Tyla would return your notebook. But she didn't, and the more you both argued, the more nervous I got. I didn't want to choose between friends."

"Sometimes you have to," I say harshly. "I didn't expect Chloe or Sophia to defend me, but you and I are in the CCSC together."

"I panic when people argue. I'm not used to it. Even when my parents were splitting up, they never argued—at least not in front of me. I want everyone to like each other."

"You want everyone to like *you*," I accuse.

"What's wrong with that? I try to find good in everyone. Even mean people have some reason why they act mean."

"Like Skeet." I remember the bully who had a crush on Becca until he moved away. "He was a total jerk."

"Not to me because I tried to understand him. He had it rough at home and no adults to help him with his anger issues."

"So what's Tyla's excuse?" I say.

"She's insecure—that's why she pretends to be perfect. But understanding her motives doesn't mean I forgive her. She was horrible to you."

"Worse than horrible." I shudder over the memory of my notebook in Tyla's hands. "I don't want to be part of any group that she's part of—even temporarily."

"It's only until the fund-raiser on Saturday. Please don't quit," Becca begs. "I'll tell Tyla she needs to apologize to you."

I arch my brow. "You'll stand up to her?"

"Yes. I swear on my kitten and all the animals in Wild Oaks and the CCSC," Becca promises. But I doubt she'll do it.

Still, we slip in the familiar rhythm of talking about random stuff like animals, clothes, and homework as we walk to our lockers. I'm complaining about my English homework (reading two chapters and writing an essay question) when I stare at my locker.

Right away, I get this weird vibe. Something's not right.

I swivel my head to look around the hall. Is someone spying on me? But I don't see anyone suspicious. Shrugging it off, I reach for my locker. As my fingers touch the lock, the metal door sags open.

"I know I shut it." I frown at Becca.

"Not tight enough," she says with a shrug.

"But I locked it, then slammed it shut."

A horrible thought jumps into my head.

I yank the door open wide. I pull out papers, textbooks, a brush, and my sweater, frantically searching—until nothing is left in my locker.

My notebook of secrets is gone.

- Chapter 11 -
A New Mystery

"Someone stole my notebook!" I frantically peer around but know it's no use. Whoever broke into my locker is long gone.

"I thought your notebook was in your backpack," Becca says.

"I didn't want anyone to take it again so I hid it beneath my sweater." I shake out my sweater and only a loose button dangles. "It's gone—and I know who took it."

"Don't jump to conclusions," Becca warns.

I ball up my sweater and toss it back into my locker. "We both know it was Tyla."

"Not for sure." She bends closer to look at my locker. "Your lock isn't broken. The thief knew your combination."

"Or had access to the office where all the locker combinations are on file," I point out. "Doesn't Tyla help out in the office during sixth period?"

"Well...yeah. But that doesn't mean she stole your notebook."

"According to the book, *Criminals and Crimes*, when someone has motive, opportunity, and means, they're the prime suspect. Check the guilty box by Tyla's name." I make a check mark in the air with my finger. "She wanted my notebook: *motive*. She works in office during sixth period, which gives her free rein of the school: *opportunity*. And when she doesn't get her way she's *mean*."

My gut twists as I imagine Tyla reading my notebook and laughing over secrets that might seem funny to her but can hurt other people.

So many secrets—and Tyla could expose them all!

I cover my face with my hands. "What am I going to do?"

"I'll help you find your notebook." Becca puts her arm around me. "If Tyla has it, I'll get it back for you."

"She's probably reading the secrets right now." I

sag against my locker. "Tyla will blab to the whole world. I'll turn on the TV news tonight and see Tyla's smug face telling a reporter about a British actor named Reggie who helped his sister steal their father's grandfather clock and hide it in our Skunk Shack."

"Not if I get to Tyla first." Becca presses her lips with determination. "She rides the bus home, so she'll be waiting in front of the school. I'll go right now."

"I'll go with you," I say.

"No." Becca wags her finger at me. "You'll only argue with her."

"I want to stomp on her like a bug and grind her into the ground until there's nothing left but bone ash and a bad smell."

"My point exactly. Wait for me at the Skunk Shack. Leo's probably there already, wondering what's taking us so long. I'll join you as soon as I can." She smiles confidently. "With your notebook."

Minutes later, I'm riding my bike up steep Wild Road. My brain whirls with my bike wheels. *Becca will get the notebook*, I think over and over, hoping it's true. But what if the secrets have already leaked into the world?

Thirty-five secrets, beginning with that fateful sleepover. I didn't tell Becca which friend invited me to that sleepover, but it's easy to guess it was Ann Marie. While her parents' divorce is a non-secret after all these years, only a few people know her parents told her at Disneyland, and rehashing that horrible time would be upsetting.

Other secrets are more explosive: Leo's real age, the drama teacher's romance with a rock star, and how Sophia got a leading role in the school play. Also, Tyla will be furious if she realizes I know where she really gets her expensive clothes and that Chloe calls her "Tyrant Tyla" behind her back.

What will Tyla do with all the secrets?

I turn into the wooded trail leading to the Skunk Shack. The trail used to be bumpy and overgrown, but since we've been using it to get to our clubhouse, the trail has smoothed out. It's peaceful in the woods with birds fluttering and chirping from high branches and slivers of sunlight shining on spring grass. I'm always a little surprised at how well the shack is hidden. Only a glint from the window hints that it's hidden beneath an umbrella of trees.

I park my bike by the table-sized stump Becca loves to sit on. Leo's mechanical gyro-board is propped nearby, and his vest is folded neatly on the stump. Why did he leave his vest outside?

Curious, I go inside the shack, but he's not there.

Bang! Thud!

I look up at the ceiling, my first thought full of panic as I envision a wild animal attack. But then I realize it must be Leo.

I run back outside and look up at the roof.

"Leo, what are you doing up there?" I call out.

His blond head peeks over the roof's edge. "Accessing solar energy through enhanced elevation."

"Huh?" I rub my forehead. "Can't you just talk like a normal kid?"

"Why would I want to?" He squints at me like I'm the weird one. "I climbed up here for sunshine." He leans farther over the edge, hanging by one hand while he shows me a thick metal dish with dozens of tiny wheels on the bottom and weird black bumps covering the top. "This is my latest surveillance tool. I call it FRODO."

I loved his bird drone, key spider, and dragon drone, but this invention looks as dull as a dinner plate. "Frodo? Like from *Lord of the Rings*?"

"Of course not," he scoffs. "It's an acronym for futuristic robotic odor detection operative. FRODO navigates targets through olfactory sensors."

Understanding Leo's techno-speak is like talking to an alien from another planet. "But why do you have it on the roof?"

"I told you—to access the sun. Its operational system is powered by solar energy. I'll come down and show you." Leo disappears over the roof. Footsteps clatter, then there's a *thunk* as Leo jumps to the ground. Holding FRODO under one arm, he takes a comb from his pocket and smooths back his mussed hair, then looks around. "Where's Becca?"

"Confronting a tyrant."

"What?" he asks as we walk into the shack.

"It's complicated." The door thuds when I close it behind me. "But when Becca comes back, the crisis should be over."

"Crisis?" He sets down his robotic wheeled plate and comes over beside me. "Is there something I can do?"

I go over to the table and sink into my wobbly chair. "No."

"Don't underestimate me." Leo gives me a look much too wise for someone only eleven years old. "If you need help, I'm here for you, Kelsey."

The gentle way he says my name cracks through my controlled emotions. Leo and I argue most of the time so his offer means a lot. Fear and worry swell in me, and I cover my face with my hands to hide my teary eyes.

"I'm not crying," I say quickly.

"Of course you are. It's natural." Leo grabs a tissue from a box on the shelf and hands it to me. "According to statistics, women spend sixteen months of their lives crying."

"That's sexist."

"It's a fact." He shrugs, looking more human than usual in a wrinkled shirt with no vest. "But if it makes you feel any better, women live longer than men."

"Good to know." I smile.

He hands me another tissue.

"Thanks, Leo," I say, sniffling. "You're a real friend."

"Yes, I am." He nods. "So tell me what's wrong."

"I never should have brought my notebook to school...Now everything's all messed up." My tears start to flow again.

Next thing I know, I'm telling him about the missing notebook.

"Oh, *that* notebook." He pulls up his chair beside me. "I saw that Sparkler girl waving it at lunch and wondered what the shouting was about. Frankie and I were going to see if you needed help, but your jock friends got there first."

"Ann Marie and Tori made Tyla give back my notebook. I put it in my locker to keep it safe—and it was stolen." I crumple the soggy tissue and toss it in the trash. "Becca *has* to get it back or secrets won't be secret anymore, which will hurt my family and friends. Everyone will hate me."

"I won't," Leo says. He has no idea that one of the secrets is his.

While we wait for Becca, Leo shows me FRODO. Up close it looks like a Frisbee dotted with odd bumps and over a dozen tiny wheels with heavy treads.

"FRODO could be a breakthrough in cyber-netics!" His voice rises with excitement. "The bumps on FRODO are powerful smell receptors made of frog eggs."

"Frog eggs? Yuck." I wrinkle my nose. "Robots can't smell."

"FRODO's olfactory system is programmed to recognize chemical signatures like blood and sweat. According to my calculations, FRODO will be able to analyze data, then determine the direction an odor is coming from."

"Like a follow-the-stink GPS?" I giggle.

"Close enough." Leo rolls his eyes.

I bend to study the frog-egged robot. "Can FRODO search and rescue like a dog?" I ask.

"Not yet." Leo fidgets with the remote control in his hand. "At this early stage his range is minimal compared to a bloodhound that can trace a scent for more than a mile."

"How far can FRODO smell?"

"Thirty-one feet," he admits. "But I'm working on it."

"Cool invention."

"Frankie came up with the idea. He'd be an asset to our club." Leo gives me a hopeful look that I ignore. I'm all for FRODO, but not so much Frankie.

I hear the whirl of a bike. "Becca's here!" I cry as I rush outside.

Becca jumps off her bike. I look at her hopefully.

"Did you find it?"

She spreads out her empty hands. "Sorry, Kelsey."

I sink down to the stump. "My life is over."

"I asked Tyla to give me the notebook. But she just looked at me like I was crazy and said, 'What notebook?' She swore she didn't take it. She even let me search her backpack and it wasn't there."

"She's too clever to carry it around."

"But she sounded genuine."

"And you believed her?" I scoff.

Becca kicks her leopard-striped sneakers against the stump, hanging her head miserably. "I don't know what to believe."

"Tyla will hurt lots of people if she exposes their secrets."

Leo comes over to stand beside us. "This sounds like a mystery for the CCSC."

"No mystery." I press my lips stubbornly. "I know who's guilty."

"Maybe." Becca bites her frosted pink lip.

Leo twirls his remote control in his fingers like a baton. "All suspects are innocent until proven guilty." He gestures to the Skunk Shack. "Let's go inside to formulate plans for recovering the notebook."

Sometimes Leo's logical way of analyzing every-thing is annoying, but being logical is better than panicking.

Leo props his electronic notebook on the lopsided table and types while I talk. I describe the events starting from when I realized I'd accidentally taken my notebook to school and ending with its being stolen. I finish by saying, "My locker door fell open because Tyla didn't lock it after she stole my notebook."

"You don't know for sure it was her," Becca argues, but her voice is quiet like she isn't so sure anymore.

"Who else?" I fold my arms to my chest. "Tyla did it."

Becca frowns at me. "Anyone who heard the argument in the cafeteria could have a motive to steal the notebook."

"Good point, Becca." Leo nods. "Someone with a guilty conscience might worry you've found out their secret."

Becca's ponytail flops to one side as she tilts her head toward me. "How many people did you write about?"

I pause, counting on my fingers. "Over thirty."

"An abundance of suspects." Leo taps his chin thoughtfully. "We'll need to decrease the number of potential suspects so I can calculate who has the highest probability of guilt."

"Tyla," I repeat with no doubt.

"Other kids, teachers, and cafeteria workers saw the notebook too," Becca says.

"I guess." I shrug. "A lot of the secrets in my notebook are about friends and family who don't go to our school. That will shorten the list."

"Kelsey, I hate to ask you this." Becca looks me straight in the eyes. "But we need to know who you wrote about."

"I can't tell you." I shake my head so adamantly that my wobbly chair almost topples over.

"I'm not asking to know the secrets—just who they're about." Becca softens her voice. "I already know one is about me."

Leo snorts with disapproval. "Kelsey, why would you write about Becca?"

"It's not about her—someone she knows." I gulp, then blurt out, "But there is one about you."

"Me?" Leo's eyes darken like a stormy sea. "Impossible."

I stare directly into his blue eyes and speak

carefully, "I know *why* you don't like birthday parties."

"How can anyone *not* like birthday parties?" Becca asks.

Leo doesn't answer, his shocked gaze fixed on me.

To prove I know his age, I hold up one finger on each hand.

His mouth falls open, but then he quickly says, "I make a motion that finding Kelsey's notebook is the CCSC's top priority."

I second this motion. And Becca's third makes it unanimous.

For the next hour, we work on the list. It's hard to remember all the names, but I come up with a dozen "suspects" who go to our school, including two teachers and the groundskeeper, Mr. Thompson.

When I'm finished, I read from the list. "Suspect Number One: Tyla. There are also secrets about Sophia, Chloe, Ann Marie, Tori, and Leo—" I pause to look apologetically at him, then continue. "Erik Taylor, Trevor Auslin, and Vince Jackson. A few adults are on the list too: Mrs. Ross, Ms. Grande, and Mr. Thompson."

"Mr. Thompson?" Becca swivels in her chair to

stare at me. "He reminds me of Hagrid with his beard and gentle smile. He's too nice to have a dark secret."

"Not all secrets are dark." I think of the million dollars that Mr. Thompson won on a reality show several years ago. It's cool he keeps quiet about his wealth and works hard instead of living off his winnings.

"Twelve names." Leo finishes typing onto his tablet. "But only eleven are suspects because obviously I'm not guilty."

"Are you sure?" Becca teases.

"Absolutely," Leo says in total seriousness.

Becca chuckles, then turns to me with a thoughtful expression. "Kelsey, if we're going to solve this mystery, Leo should know what you wrote about him."

"I think he already does." I raise my brows in question toward Leo.

"As George Orwell wrote in his book *1984*," Leo says, not meeting my gaze, "*if you want to keep a secret, you must also hide it from yourself.*"

"So hidden it will stay," I say with some relief.

We pack up our stuff and leave the clubhouse. Even though it's getting late, I don't want to go home without visiting my kitten. Leo comes along too, zooming ahead of our bikes on his gyro-board.

We ride down the steep hill and past animal outbuildings, hearing roars and screeches and birds calling to each other. I usually feel a thrill whenever I'm around all these amazing animals. All I can feel now is anxiety...but that shifts to curiosity when I see a large moving van parked in front of Becca's house.

"Mom didn't mention a delivery." Becca picks up her pace.

"It must be something big—like furniture?" Leo guesses.

I grin. "Or an elephant."

"The van's big enough for a dinosaur," Becca jokes.

We reach the truck just as Becca's mother comes out the front door and approaches a man in a dark-brown delivery uniform.

Mrs. Morales frowns at the man. "I didn't order anything."

"You got one anyway. Must be your lucky day." The burly man checks his clipboard. "From a Mr. R. Sinclair to Becca, Kelsey, and Leo."

"Becca?" Mrs. Morales narrows her gaze at her daughter. "What's this about?"

"Absolutely *no* idea." Becca shakes her head so adamantly her ponytail flops. "I didn't order anything."

"So you're Becca?" the deliveryman asks, tapping his pen against the clipboard impatiently.

She nods. "But I don't know a Mr. Sinclair."

"Well, the dude knows you." The deliveryman thrusts the clipboard and a pen at Becca, and then he strides around to the rear of the truck and calls out, "Where do you want your tortoise?"

- Chapter 12 -
Shell-Shocked

"Albert!" I exclaim, as a leathery head peeks out of snug blankets. He's mummy-wrapped in thick blankets inside a shallow, giant metal tub, like an industrial version of a kiddie pool.

"I can't take a tortoise—especially one so big," Mrs. Morales protests, throwing up her arms. "My goodness, he must weigh over five hundred pounds."

"Four hundred and seventy-three pounds," the deliveryman says, checking some papers. "But I've hauled heavier cargo. No idea why you weren't informed of the delivery, but this letter might explain things." He hands her a plain white envelope.

Mrs. Morales glances down. "It isn't addressed to me."

Becca's ponytail flops as she leans to read over her mother's shoulder. "Who's it for?"

"You kids." Mrs. Morales points to us.

"No way!" Becca's forehead creases in uncertainty as she accepts the letter. She skims it, then looks up at us.

"It's from Reggie." She bites her lip. "Oh no. This is *not* good."

"What's he say?" I ask.

"Read it out loud," Leo urges.

Becca swallows nervously, then begins to read:

Hey, Kids,

Surprised to hear from me? Since our visit, a lot has happened!

I told you I was an actor, but mostly I'm an out-of-work actor. Living so far north of LA, I can't make many auditions. When I do audition, I have to hurry back to Albert.

My family is big on tradition so when my parents moved back to England, they left

Albert in my care. Berty and I have had a smashing run together, but now I have the offer of a lifetime for a role in a major movie. I can't pass this up-even though it means moving to LA.

Wild Oaks Sanctuary will be a great home for Albert. I'll miss the old fellow terribly, but I just can't keep him now. He gets depressed when he's alone, so I couldn't leave him at my house. He needs to be around people, and he's great with other animals too. You kids got on brilliantly with Albert, and I trust you to care for him.

Attached is a list of Albert's favorite foods and care instructions.

I'll contact you once I'm settled in LA.

With sincere regards,
Reginald Alexander Sinclair

Paper rustles as Becca lowers her hand and looks up at her mother. "Uh, I guess we have a tortoise."

Mrs. Morales is still arguing with the deliveryman as they walk around to the back of the truck.

"I'm just doing my job, ma'am." The deliveryman shakes his head.

"I know, which adds to my frustration because I want to yell at someone and this isn't your fault." Her gaze shifts to us, her shoulders rigid with anger. "The tortoise can stay in the Bird Island enclosure. I'll get one of my volunteers, Hank, to help move him."

"I'll help," Becca offers.

"You wait here. Hank and I will handle this." Mrs. Morales rakes her fingers through her curly dark hair. "We'll talk once the tortoise is settled."

"So Albert can stay?" Becca asks hopefully.

"Temporarily." She glares daggers at Becca. "I let you keep two small kittens, but a giant tortoise is a huge responsibility. Call your actor friend and tell him to get back here because we can*not* keep a five-hundred-pound tortoise."

"Four hundred and seventy-three pounds," Leo corrects.

"You're not helping," I whisper to Leo.

"I have enough to deal with without a giant reptile!" Mrs. Morales throws up her hands and mutters something in Spanish as she stomps over to the deliveryman.

"Your mom's really mad." I shudder.

"Yeah." Becca gnaws on the end of her ponytail. "She's stressed because the Humane Society fund-raiser is only five days away and she has to prepare the animals that will be on display. A bunch of volunteers will help out at the fund-raiser, but Hank's the only one here regularly and I can't help on school days."

"We have to convince her to let Albert stay permanently," Leo says, balancing his gyro-board on one end while he stares at the delivery van.

Becca sighs. "Mom doesn't change her mind easily. Reggie shouldn't have sent him here without asking. He didn't even say if he'll come back for Reggie or if he wants us to keep him for good. And why give him to us instead of someone in his family?"

"His grandmother can't keep Albert at an apartment, and his parents are in England," I remind her.

"But why not his sister?" Leo taps his finger to

his chin thoughtfully. "I suspect Reggie isn't telling us something."

"Obviously there's a lot we don't know." Becca frowns at the grinding sound of a hydraulic lift coming from Bird Island. "It would be coolness to keep Albert, and I might have been able to convince Mom if Reggie told me his plans first. When we talked about the sanctuary, I had no idea he'd give us his tortoise."

"A rare and valuable reptile," Leo adds. "According to my calculations, Albert is worth as much as $30,000 today on the private pet market."

"Wow!" Becca gives a low whistle.

"We really have to talk to Reggie," I say. "Did he leave a phone number?"

Becca checks the letter, then shakes her head. "No number. How do we get in touch with him?"

"I'll search online. I can search more efficiently on my home computer, so I'll go there now." Leo jumps on his gyro-board. "I'll text when I find out Reggie's number."

"Not so fast, Leo." I move in front of his gyro-board, my hands on my hips. "What about *my* notebook? It's supposed to be CCSC top priority. You know how important it is to get it back."

"Very important." Leo nods solemnly. "I'll work on both things when I get home. I'll let you know tomorrow at school what I find out."

"Tomorrow may be too late. The thief—or, as I like to refer to her, Tyla—will have spilled all the secrets online—if she hasn't already."

Leo goes pale and I'm sure he's thinking about his secret.

"I'll check now," Becca offers, taking her phone from her pocket. "I know Tyla's favorite sites." After a few minutes of tap-tapping on her phone, Becca looks up at us. "I can't find any recent posts from Tyla. No news is good news."

"Until the bad news hits the fan," I say ominously. "Why hasn't Tyla blasted all the secrets yet?"

"Because she's innocent," Becca insists.

"If she doesn't have my notebook, she knows who does."

"Kelsey Case, you're the most stubborn person ever!" Becca flips her ponytail behind her shoulder. "Once you get an idea, it's stuck like superglue. But consider this for a moment: What if you're wrong about Tyla?"

"I'm not stubborn," I say stubbornly. "I just know Tyla is guilty."

"Then I'll have to prove she isn't." Becca blows out a heavy sigh. "I was hoping I wouldn't have to do this."

"What?" Leo and I both ask.

"Tyla asked me to come to her house after school tomorrow to practice face-painting designs."

I frown. "You're going there instead of meeting us at the Skunk Shack?"

"I wasn't going to, but now I will so I can look in her room for the notebook. I know her hiding places. If she has the notebook, I'll find it."

"You'll spy on a friend for me?" I ask, touched.

"I don't feel good about it." Becca sighs. "But yeah, I'll do it."

"Text me if you find anything. I'll see you tomorrow." Leo clicks the remote to his gyro-board, then zooms away, gravel spitting from his wheels.

"I guess I should go too," I say, standing up from the porch swing. "Unless you want me to stay for support. Your mom sounded really mad."

"I can handle her," Becca says with a smile. "Go on. I'll see you tomorrow."

As I bike away, I feel guilty for leaving Becca. But she didn't seem worried, so I guess I shouldn't be either. Hopefully, Mrs. Morales will calm down once Becca explains that it's not her fault Reggie gave us the tortoise.

I can't help Becca, but I can try to help lost pets.

So as I pedal home, I detour through side streets, on the lookout.

When I hear a bark, I glance around until I spot a rottweiler in a fenced front yard. I love seeing a happy dog safe in his yard. So many pets get lost like runaway Bobbsey. With so much else going on, I forgot to tell Becca and Leo about spotting the dog in Galena Park.

Pets—like criminals in mysteries—often return to the scene of the crime. I head to the park where I last saw Bobbsey. I've started carrying around dog treats and a leash in my backpack, so if I can get close to him, he won't get away this time.

But I ride through the park three times and there's no sign of the blue-eyed healer. Discouraged, I ride slowly home, then lock my bike in the apartment rack and trudge up the stairs.

I'm surprised when the door opens before I can turn the knob.

"Kelsey, about time you got home," Mom says but she's smiling. And she looks so professional in her animal control officer uniform.

"Am I late for dinner?"

"No, but I've been waiting for you." She puts her arm around my shoulders and ushers me into the living room where we sit on the couch. She reaches for a stack of papers on the coffee table and hands them to me. "For you and your friends. Since you've recovered some lost pets, I thought you'd like these."

Missing pet flyers—hot off the press!

"Wow, thanks, Mom!" I give her a hug, then eagerly flip through six flyers.

Right on the top is an updated flyer for Bobbsey. His reward is now fifty dollars. The remaining flyers are for an elderly Siamese cat named Hugo, a pug named Pugsley, and a dachshund named Ditzy that I recognize because he was lost once before until Becca and I returned him. The flyer says that he escaped from a locked yard. *A repeat offender*, I think with a wry smile.

Becca and Leo will be pleased when I tell them we won't have to go online for lost pet news—I have an informant at home.

During dinner, Mom is the center of the Case family universe. She tells us about meeting the other employees, touring the buildings, and reuniting owners with missing pets. I know there are unpleasant duties too, but it's her first day so I don't ask.

Becca calls as I'm getting ready for bed. I take the phone into my room, shutting the door firmly.

"Hey, Becca." I keep my voice low because the walls are thin and my sisters are in the next room. "Is your mom still mad about Albert?"

"Mom doesn't blame me, but she's stressed to the max. She says Albert could get sick if he stays with the birds very long. He needs to have his own water pond, but there aren't funds to build him a safe enclosure."

"It can't be that expensive," I say. "We could help with our CCSC money. This would be a good cause to donate to."

"It would take hundreds of dollars—we don't have enough." Becca sounds so discouraged that I imagine her twisting her ponytail. "I thought a tortoise would be easy to care for—until I read Reggie's list. It doesn't just list all the foods Albert can and can't eat. He also has to have an insulated building to sleep in that's temperature controlled."

"Really?" I ask, surprised.

"Aldabra tortoises are cold-blood reptiles and

can't heat themselves. Also, Albert doesn't drink from a water bowl so he needs his own watering hole. Similar to what we have for the alligator— but it's not like they can share the same enclosure."

"Tortoise soup," I joke.

"Not funny." Becca groans. "Reggie's instructions say Albert needs to be near a mulberry tree so he can stretch his neck to eat leaves. He needs interesting things in his pen so he gets exercise because he could get depressed if he's bored. And the list goes on for *three pages!*"

Becca is shouting now, so I pull the phone away from my ear.

She takes a deep breath, then adds that she talked with Tyla and is going to her house tomorrow after school.

"Did Tyla say anything about my notebook?"

"Yeah. It was really awkward." Becca pauses so long that I wonder if she hung up until she sighs.

"What happened?"

"Tyla said I betrayed our friendship and hurt her feelings when I accused her of being a thief. I felt awful. I was going to apologize until I remembered how horrible she was to you. So I told her it was her fault for taking your notebook at lunch."

"You did?" If I wasn't holding the phone, I would applaud. Becca is finally standing up to Tyla!

"It wasn't easy but it felt good. Tyla said she was teasing and swore she didn't have your notebook."

"She never admits being wrong." I squeeze a pillow behind my back. "Do you believe her?"

"I don't know...but if she has it, she'll return it soon. I'll bet that your notebook will be in your locker when you get to school tomorrow."

"I hope so," I say softly, then hang up and click off my bed lamp. I fall asleep imagining myself walking down the school hall, opening my locker, and there's my notebook.

When I wake up the next morning, I can't wait to get to school to check my locker. Riding through the school gates, I quickly lock up my bike in the rack, then hurry to my locker.

My hand trembles as I reach for the combination lock. I spin the dial so fast I mess up the numbers and have to start over. I hold my breath as the lock clicks open.

I open my door and stare inside.

There is something!

And I gasp.

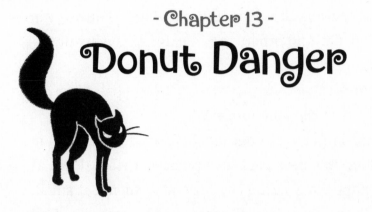

- Chapter 13 -
Donut Danger

I reach into my locker and pull out a folded sheet of pale-yellow paper. I open it up and read:

Look 4 📓.

Go 2 Donut D-Lite at 3:15 alOne.

🍩 Tell anyOne.

(👁 aM wAtching U.)

It looks like something a little kid would make in art class: jumbled words and pictures glued across scraps of paper like a collage. Some are in bold print, and others are in color or in tiny newspaper print.

OMG!

My first ransom note ever!

I'm desperate to get my notebook back but I'm thrilled too, because I love puzzles. I stare down at the paper, wrinkling my nose at a chemical smell, like hair spray mixed with mouthwash. The first part of the note is easy. The notebook thief wants to meet at Donut D-Lite at 3:15, and I have to come alone. The donut picture confuses me at first until I realize it's a pun. Donut = Do Not. *Do not.* So I'm not supposed to tell anyone. The paper eye watching me is creepy. Is it warning that if I don't come alone or tell someone I'll never see my notebook again?

But why isn't there a ransom demand?

Usually a ransomer (is that even a word?) asks for money or for something in exchange. At least that's how it works in books and on TV. But all the notebook thief asks is for me to go to a donut shop after school, which sounds kind of yummy.

Why would Tyla leave a cryptic message instead

of the notebook? And why work so hard cutting and pasting a do-it-yourself ransom note instead of printing one from her computer?

Studying the paper, I'm troubled by the "do not tell anyone" line. Assuming it's from Tyla, why does she want me to keep it a secret? Is it because she doesn't want Becca to find out?

When Becca arrives a few minutes later, I'm so tempted to show her the note. But I imagine the eyeball in the note spying on me. And I don't want to lose my chance to get back my notebook. So I slip the ransom note into my backpack.

"Sooo?" Becca gestures to my locker, then looks at me hopefully. "Was it there?"

I hang my head. "No notebook."

"Kelsey, I'm so sorry." Becca gives my hand a squeeze. "If Tyla had the notebook, your secrets would already be blasted across the World Wide Web. But I checked her social sites and nada."

"She's keeping quiet to torture me—and it's working."

"We'll find it," Becca assures me. "I'll go home with Tyla after school and check under her bed— that's where she usually puts important stuff. But I really don't think it will be there."

A startling thought hits me: I may be wrong about Tyla. She will be with Becca after school — at the same time I'm meeting the ransomer. Unless she can be in two places at once, she didn't steal my notebook.

"I won't be back in time for a CCSC meeting," Becca adds with a sigh. "But you can still come over to my house to see your kitten."

"I'd love to cuddle Honey, but I have other things to do."

"Leo has plans too," Becca says.

"When doesn't he?" I give a frustration gesture. "Let me guess. He's helping Frankie again?"

Becca nods. "Leo finished the giraffe and is now assembling a lion head. But he stayed up late last night digging for information and texted what he found out about Reggie."

"What?" I lower my voice in case we're being watched.

"Reggie's sister lives in Alaska — way too cold for a tortoise." Becca shivers. "Leo tried calling her to find out Reggie's phone number, but she didn't answer. He left a message and is hoping to hear back soon. I sure hope we can talk to Reggie ASAP because time is running out for Albert."

"What do you mean?" I ask, alarmed.

Becca twists her pink-streaked black ponytail. "Mom contacted a tortoise club, and they're looking for a home for him."

"But Reggie left him to us," I argue. "She can't give him away."

"She can and she will," Becca says with a heavy sigh. "Reggie needs to come back soon."

My gaze falls to my backpack. "What else did Leo find out? Anything about my notebook?"

"He doesn't know who took it, but he narrowed the suspect list to three names."

"Who?" I ask, having a good idea who tops the list.

"Erik Taylor, Sophia, and Tyla." Becca frowns. "All I know about Erik is that he plays hoops and he's a photographer for the yearbook committee. What do you know about him?"

He posts a scandalous blog under the name the Corning Comic, I think as I shut my locker with a bang. "I can't tell you his secret, but if his buddies find out about it, they'll hate him."

"It's *that* bad?" Becca leans so close her ponytail brushes my arm.

I nod. Erik's online comic strip mocks kids at our

school. He posts under "the Corning Comic" so no one knows it's him. We were partners once on an English project, and when I borrowed his notes, I found drawings for his website. No one would ever suspect he's the Corning Comic—unless they read my notebook.

"What about Sophia's secret?" Becca asks in a hushed voice. "Is it bad too?"

"Worse than Erik's" is all I'll say.

I really like Sophia so I was disappointed when I overheard her telling Tyla she had bribed Perrin Jefferson, the assistant for the drama teacher, with hard-to-get theater tickets she'd gotten as a gift so he'd help her land the role of Nala in *The Lion King*. And the bribe worked because she got the part.

"At least the thief hasn't posted the secrets online," Becca says.

"Not yet." *As long as I follow the ransom instructions.*

I glance at my watch and wonder what I'll find when I go to the donut shop. If Donut D-Lite wasn't a popular business, I'd never go alone. My dad criticizes the donuts as "fast food" (his version of the F-word), but my mother loves D-Lite donuts and shares with us kids. The donut shop is near our old house, so I know exactly how to get there.

I think about the ransom note all through my classes. Who sent it? Why leave a ransom note instead of the notebook? Will I find my notebook at D-Lite Donuts, or am I walking into a trap?

I should tell Becca and Leo where I'm going. But they'd insist on coming. I have to follow the instructions, or I may never see my notebook again.

Besides, what could be dangerous about going to a donut shop?

As soon as the final bell rings, I race to my bike and pedal away.

I'm off to meet a notebook-napper, I think with a thrill of excitement.

I ride through my old neighborhood, passing the playground I enjoyed when I was little. I had so much fun running across the tire bridge and slipping down the swan-shaped slide with Ann Marie and Tori. Ann Marie still lives next to my old house. But a new family lives in our wonderful two-story home with its big yard and tree swing. I ride past my former street without even looking.

The big, pink donut in the sky beckons. When I've

come here before—usually early in the morning—the parking lot has been packed with a line snaking out the door. But now the giant donut on the roof isn't flashing. The parking lot is empty.

I prop my bike up on the kickstand and go over to the glass front door. I peer through the window into darkness. I rattle the handle but the door is locked.

Where is everyone?

And I notice the *Closed* sign.

I read the posted hours: 5 a.m.–2 p.m.

It never occurred to me that such a popular business would close early. I'd expected lots of people and felt it was safe to come alone. I ignored the advice in *Spy Now, Die Later*: *When meeting a suspect, always have backup.*

Instead, no one knows where I am—except the thief.

The smart thing to do would be to ride away, but what about my notebook? Does the thief plan to return it, or is this a cruel prank?

I turn around in place, slowly, on the alert for anything suspicious.

A good spy assesses the situation before deciding on a course of action. Assuming the thief is one of our suspects, it's unlikely he or she is inside a closed business. But there are no cars or even a bike in the parking lot, only a trash can and a garden shed.

Waiting around is boring. Waiting for an unknown thief is risky. The smart thing to do would be to leave *now*. But I really, really want my notebook.

So I straddle my bike, my sneaker toes poised to kick off at the first hint of trouble. Glancing down at my watch, I watch seconds tick by into minutes.

By three thirty, I'm fuming inside. This whole ransom-note drama is a prank. No one is coming. I'm pretty sure the thief (gimme a guilty T-Y-L-A) is laughing while she has fun hanging out with Becca.

Still, what if my notebook is here?

I can't search inside the store, but I can check around the building. I leave my bike and walk along the paved walkway circling the donut shop. I peer into bushes, behind a flower planter, and beneath a stone bench.

No notebook.

I walk around the back of the building to the dumpster. The lid is pushed back, showing plastic bags piled taller than me, some ripped open with trash spilling down to the concrete.

A few weeks ago, Becca, Leo, and I rescued kittens from a dumpster in a creepy alley. This dumpster smells and looks worse. Do I want my notebook badly enough to search through piles of trash?

The stench of decaying food and sour milk turns my stomach. Searching through dozens of trash bags would take hours and make a huge mess. So I just search around the dumpster. I'm pushing aside a trash bag covered in donut sprinkles when I hear an odd noise.

Whirling around, I don't see anyone.

I start to turn back to the trash when there's a *thud*.

And this time I can tell where it's coming from— inside the shed at the back of the parking lot. It's a small metal shed, probably used for tools and storage.

I hear the thud again. And another sound, soft and plaintive...like a moan.

OMG! Something alive is inside the shed!

I stare ahead, holding my arms around myself so I don't freak out.

When I hear a whimper, I worry that someone is bleeding or dying. And it's up to me to save them.

But then I think of horror movies where zombies and monsters burst out of dark places. Should I run to the shed to help?

Or should I run away?

I finally decide the safest thing to do is find an adult who can help. I turn around and start for my bike...but stop when I hear the whimper again.

The sound clicks in my head.

I know that whimper!

Instead of fleeing for my own safety, I race forward. When I reach the shed, I lift the metal latch, surprised but relieved it's not locked. The door slides open with a scraping sound.

Blue eyes gleam dangerously at me from the darkness.

- Chapter 14 -

Puzzling

"Bobbsey!" I cry, then soften my tone as I repeat his name in a soothing way that won't frighten him.

The dog quivers in the shadows. His bobbed tail wags so I'm sure he won't bite me. Still I don't make any sudden moves, taking one step forward with my hand outstretched so he can smell me and know I'm a friend.

Whining, Bobbsey cowers and backs away. I stand very still while I try to figure out how to catch him. If I grab and miss, he'll run out the open door behind me.

Keeping my gaze focused on Bobbsey, I reach back with one hand and feel for the door latch. I don't want to shut the door completely—that would leave us both in the dark. I need to close it enough to block him from escaping. My fingers slide around a metal handle. I pull slowly, light dimming to only a crack in the door. I call Bobbsey soothingly by his name to hide any noise the door might make.

With the door open a few inches, sunlight streams behind me. As my eyes adjust, shadowed shapes become clearer. This is a garden shed with a rake, a hoe, a ladder, a wheelbarrow, and coils of hose. Nothing I can use to catch a scared dog.

"It's okay, Bobbsey," I murmur, bending my knees so I seem shorter than usual and less threatening.

He whines but lifts his head, his blue eyes shining eagerly. I can tell he wants to come over to me. This is exactly why I started carrying about a leash and dog treats in my backpack. Moving slowly and keeping my gaze on the dog, I feel around in my backpack until I find the dog treats.

When I lift the steak-flavored one, Bobbsey jumps to his paws. He barks and wiggles his stubby tail.

"It's all yours, boy." I hold the treat closer so the savory smell breezes in the small shed, making me a little hungry. Not that I'd resort to eating dog treats...Well, not unless I was stranded and starving.

It takes two more doggie snacks to gain Bobbsey's trust.

"Good boy," I say as I scratch behind his ears with one hand and click the leash onto his collar with the other.

I start to lead him out of the shed when I slap my palm to my head. Duh! I almost left without searching for my notebook. Did someone trap the dog to lure me in here so I would find my notebook? Or is finding Bobbsey a coincidence? The only thing I know for sure is that Bobbsey didn't shut himself inside this shed.

The shed isn't big so it doesn't take long to discover my notebook isn't here. It wasn't near the Donut D-Lite building or in the parking lot. And I doubt it's inside the dumpster—why toss something worth ransoming in the garbage?

But why would someone claim to have the notebook and then not show up?

I shake my head, frustrated. No point in searching for something that was never here. It's what I *did* find that matters. And I smile down at Bobbsey. "Your owner is going to be so happy to see you!"

Bobbsey nudges his head against my leg. "Ready to go home?"

He barks and I chuckle. "Okay, boy, let's figure out where you live."

Holding the leash with one hand, I dig into my backpack for the Lost Pet flyers, then flip through them for Bobbsey's contact information: 1933 Larkspur Lane. Hmmm, that sounds familiar. Maybe the new gated community near Riverview Hill? It's on the south end of town. There's a phone number too, which would be great if I had a phone.

But I know where I can borrow one. I'm only a few blocks away from my old house. So I head for Ann Marie's house.

Leading a timid dog home while riding my bike would be a bad idea. If he suddenly bolted, I could end up on the pavement and he'd be gone again. So I walk my bike while leading Bobbsey on the leash. (Apparently he loves to walk.) I know Ann Marie won't be home since she has some kind of sport practice every afternoon, but her mother (who considers me her second daughter) is thrilled to see me.

"Kelsey! It's been so long!" she cries, wrapping me in a hug so tight that I gasp for air.

When she lets me up for air, I explain about

finding Bobbsey, then ask to use her phone to call his owner.

It's a quick call. Bobbsey's elderly owner sounds feeble—until I tell him why I'm calling. Then his voice rises with excitement like a kid surprised with a birthday party. I give him the address, and he says he's coming right away.

While I wait, Mrs. Sanchez sits me down at the kitchen table and insists on making me a sandwich, just like when I was little. She feeds Bobbsey too. Mrs. Sanchez hasn't changed at all, which makes me smile.

"Nice dog," she says. "He still looks hungry though. I'll see what I can find for him." As she turns to search the fridge, she rambles on about her job at the hospital and shows me Ann Marie's latest athletic trophies. Ann Marie is an only child—which I've often envied. I love my family, but sometimes it would be nice to be an "only" and not wait my turn for new clothes or to use the computer.

Mrs. Sanchez wants to know everything about my family. So I tell her about Dad's baking masterpieces, how cool Mom looked in her animal control officer uniform, Kyle's determination to get a college scholarship, and how my sisters are so popular and busy I rarely see them.

I'm telling her how I ride around looking for lost pets when the doorbell rings. Mrs. Sanchez sets down her steaming coffee cup and then excuses herself to answer the door.

"Bobbsey," I tell the dog sitting at my feet, "I think your owner is here. He sounded so excited on the phone and can't wait to see you."

The owner, Mr. Sudbury, doesn't have much hair on his head, but his wiry gray beard goes down to his chubby chest. When he sees Bobbsey, his eyes redden as he sniffles. Opening his arms he runs forward, meeting Bobbsey halfway, and their hug is so sweet I feel a little emotional too.

Mr. Sudbury thanks me at least twenty times, then insists that I take the fifty-dollar reward.

"It'll go toward helping other animals. Thank you so much," I tell the old man, but he's clicking a leash onto Bobbsey's collar. A few minutes later they're gone.

I don't stay much longer either.

After hugs and promises to visit more often, I put on my bike helmet and then ride off.

I'm smiling as I think about how great it felt to reunite Bobbsey with his owner, but after a few blocks my smile fades with thoughts of my missing notebook.

Was it a coincidence that I found Bobbsey at D-Lite Donuts? Or was he purposely left there for me to find? But why leave a pet instead of my notebook?

It doesn't make any sense.

When I get home, I spread the ransom note under a bright light on my desk and look for clues. The thief was careful not to use their own handwriting, only cutout words and images from magazines. I doubt there are any fingerprints, but I take my spy pack from the closet, slip on gloves, and sprinkle graphic powder across the paper. I find several clear prints—all mine.

Pulling out my magnifying glass, I examine each glued piece of paper. They're mostly from magazines with colorful printing formats. The donut could be from any food magazine—Dad has a cupboard full in the kitchen. The phrase "meet me" has a loose corner that I pull up gently until it comes off. On the other side of the paper there's a cartoon of a clown with half of his face smiling and the other half frowning.

Hmmm…that's familiar. But I can't think of where I've seen it before.

I stick the weird face picture back on the paper, the glue still strong enough to hold it in place. My nose and eyes itch at a strong chemical odor. I sniff and the smell is definitely coming from the paper, sort of like a detergent mixed with flowers.

I'm on the scent of a clue—literally!

I dig my fingernail at the edge of the eyeball paper until it lifts off. My eyes itch again and the smell increases. I fight the urge to sneeze as I stare down at the paper eyeball in my hand. It's slick and glossy like it came from a magazine.

Curious, I flip it over, and in bold print is the name of a popular magazine: *InbeTWEEN*. My sisters used to read the trendy teen-zine and cut out photos of cute guys. Now instead of ogling airbrushed guys, they're going out with high school guys.

My sisters stopped reading *InbeTWEEN* two years ago, so why do I have a memory of seeing the magazine recently?

Not at school or at home.

Memory slams into me, and I suck in a sharp breath.

I saw *InbeTWEEN* magazine in Becca's bedroom.

- Chapter 15 -
The Corning Comic

A coincidence, of course.

Becca would never steal from me or leave a ransom note.

But she might know which of our suspects reads *InbeTWEEN*. It's too late to call her so I'll ask her tomorrow at school—if I can get her alone. I should have told my club mates about the ransom note instead of keeping it a secret. With Becca's social savvy and Leo's analytical deductions, we'd have probably found my notebook by now—or at least know who took it.

Will I get it back before secrets are exposed?

The next morning, I find out.

I arrive at school early and am spinning the

combo of my locker when I hear, "Kelsey! Kelsey!"

Whirling around, I see Becca pounding down the hall in tiger-striped sneakers, her ponytail flopping behind her like a pink flame in black smoke.

"OMG—the worst has happened!" Becca cries as she comes up beside me, bending slightly to catch her breath.

I tense. "What?"

"One of your secrets has gone viral!"

"*No!*" I stare at her in horror. "How do you know it's one of mine?"

"It's about Sophia and it's really bad." Becca drops her voice dramatically as she shows me her phone screen. "Check this out."

I'm afraid to look, but I do.

My breath catches as I recognize the Corning Comic website. The site created by one of our top three suspects.

Secret 23 flashes like a disaster headline across my mind: Erik Taylor anonymously posts a snarky web comic strip mocking other students under the name "the Corning Comic."

Becca clicks a link, then shows a photo of Sophia in a lion costume similar to the one Frankie created for her Nala role. The caption reads: *The Lying Queen.*

"OMG!" I reach out to hold myself steady against my locker.

"Sophia must be devastated." Becca sighs. "I feel awful for her."

I feel awful too as I read the comic strip, which uses cute drawings to accuse Sophia of having no talent and bribing Perrin Jefferson to get the lead role.

"Is this the secret you had about Sophia?" Becca asks.

What's the point in lying now? The secret is out. So I nod.

"I just can't believe it." Becca spreads out her hands, and her silver bracelets jangle like a sad song. "Why would Sophia cheat? And how could you know about this and say nothing?"

"It's easier to keep the secret than to hurt a friend." I sigh. "Sophia is really sweet and never says anything mean about anyone."

"She didn't have to bribe Perrin—she deserved that role. She's talented with an amazing singing voice. The Corning Comic got that wrong." Becca taps her phone screen. "I'm worried about her. She's super sensitive and must be devastated. I've texted her but she won't answer."

"It's all my fault," I groan. "If I hadn't been so careless and brought my notebook to school, Sophia's secret would still be secret."

Becca pats my shoulder. "How did you find out about it?"

My face reddens because my answer is almost as humiliating as Sophia's secret. "I was in a school bathroom stall...um...sitting. Sophia came in with Tyla, and they were at the sinks talking about the play. I didn't even mean to eavesdrop—I just have this weird luck when it comes to discovering secrets. Tyla said she was surprised Sophia got the Nala role instead of Sonali Ma—" I pause trying to remember her last name.

"Sonali Malhotra," Becca tells me. "Gorgeous eighth grader with amazing black hair that goes down past her waist. She usually gets the female lead in our school plays but not this time."

"Because Sophia got it." I glance up, then down the hall and whisper, "Sophia told Tyla she wanted to play Nala so much that when Perrin Jefferson— the drama teacher's assistant—bragged that he could influence the drama teacher, Sophia gave him theater tickets so he'd help her get the role."

"Bribe!" Becca says this so loudly that she claps

her hand over her mouth, then lowers her voice. "I never liked Perrin—he acts like he's important and is totally fake. Mrs. Ross seems to trust him but I don't believe he can influence her. She makes her own decisions about acting roles."

"Sophia got the role of Nala," I point out with a shrug.

"Why isn't Perrin on our suspect list?" Becca raises her dark brows.

"The secret was about Sophia—although I guess it's his secret too." I stare off down the hall, not seeing any of the kids hurrying to class, only pages in a stolen notebook. This secret was bad, but others are worse.

"Well, we can cross Sophia off Leo's suspect list," Becca says. "She wouldn't steal your notebook and then tell everyone her own secret. The Corning Comic is the top suspect—whoever he or she is."

He's already on the list.

Erik Taylor, aka the Corning Comic, is looking very, very guilty.

"The Comic must have stolen your notebook to get gossip for his snarky website—and he started with Sophia." Becca balls her fists like she's ready to do battle to defend a friend. "Who will he target next?"

I frown, imagining Leo's hurt when the whole school finds out his real age. Becca will be embarrassed too, if kids tease about her mom dating the sheriff.

"We have to stop him or her," Becca adds with a furious twist of her lips. "But the coward hides behind a fake name. No one knows who he is."

"Actually...I do." I gnaw on my lip. "His identity is one of my secrets."

"And you can't tell me." Becca rolls her eyes. "But now I know it's a he."

"I shouldn't have said that."

"Stop it already! I'm tired of your secrets." Becca covers her mouth with her hand. "Sorry, I didn't mean to lose my temper. I'm just worried about Sophia."

"I'm worried about her too," I say softly.

"Then don't protect the Corning Comic. Leo and I need to know who he is if you want us to help find your notebook."

I glance down at my white sneakers, frowning at a grass stain on my toe.

"Do you want him to post more secrets?" Becca persists.

"Of course not. But if I tell one secret, I might tell

another secret, and soon all of the secrets will be out. It's sort of like trying to eat just one french fry."

"No one can do that," Becca says with a frustrated look.

"My dilemma exactly. I feel like a superhero forced to make the decision whether to save one person or an entire planet."

"I swear no planets will be destroyed if you tell me this one secret." Becca solemnly makes a "cross my heart" gesture. "Who is the Corning Comic?"

I take a deep breath, and as I blow it out, an idea pops into my head. "I'll tell you—after I talk to him."

"That slimy snake won't talk to you," Becca says. "And if he does, he'll post all about it and you'll be humiliated like Sophia."

"But what if I can persuade him to take down the post about Sophia and not post any more secrets?"

"He'll never do it."

"I have to try. He's usually hanging out at the school basketball court with his buddies. I'll look for him there."

"Just shout out, 'Corning Comic!' That will get his attention."

"Or scare him off." Dread rises inside me. "He

must have been surprised to read my notebook and find out I knew he was the Comic."

Becca squeezes my hand. "Knowing his real identity is your superpower. Use it wisely."

"I just want my notebook back," I say sadly.

"This proves it wasn't stolen by a Sparkler." Becca looks relieved as we walk away from the lockers. "Leo can cross Sophia and Tyla off the suspect list. That leaves just two: Erik Taylor and the Corning Comic."

Two names but only one suspect, I think.

Clues are falling into place. Erik Taylor must have been in the cafeteria yesterday and saw Tyla waving my notebook of secrets. Afterward, he broke into my locker and stole my notebook so he could boost his web hits with dramatic secrets. It would be easy for him to piece together a ransom note—a yearbook photographer probably had lots of magazines lying around.

But some things still puzzle me. Why would Erik send me to D-Lite Donuts, then not leave the notebook? And how did Bobbsey get in the shed? Was finding him a coincidence or did Erik do that too?

When Becca's phone dings, she jumps excitedly.

"Sophia!" But after checking her phone, she sighs. "Just Leo."

Becca says Leo is in the drama supply room with Frankie. So we go there.

The auditorium is semi-dark and silent as we walk through aisles. Soft thuds from our sneakers are the only sounds as we walk up a short staircase and cross the stage to the backstage door.

A blend of unusual smells of fabric, oils, and dust fill the storage room where costumes, sets, and unusual props like a metallic giraffe are crammed together. I hear voices and wind through a passage bordered in boxes, cabinets, and a rolling cart with hanging clothes from the Victorian era.

I hear the boys before I see them and follow their voices to the "office" where Frankie has papers and mechanical parts strewn across his desk of a plywood sheet over boxes.

Leo sets down a screwdriver as he comes over to meet us. "What have you discovered?"

"Not here," I say with a tilt of my head toward Frankie, who is watching us from his desk. The blue streak in his dark hair waves across his forehead, and his eyes are shadowed by his green cap.

"You can talk in front of Frankie," Leo assures

us. "He knows a lot about what goes on at school and can be a great help."

"This doesn't concern him," I say.

"Does it have something to do with the Corning Comic?" Frankie guesses, unfolding tall and lanky like a marionette come to life. He gives us a friendly smile, but there's something guarded in his expression.

"What do you know about the Comic?" I ask.

Frankie frowns. "I saw the cartoon this morning, and it sucks for Sophia. Sure, she bosses me around like the other drama kids do, but she always thanks me or sometimes just comes in to talk. I feel bad for her."

"What cartoon?" Leo wrinkles his brow.

"Here." Becca holds out her phone.

"No one knows who the Corning Comic is," Frankie adds, untwisting a tangle of wires. "It's the biggest mystery at school."

Becca raises her brows at me, but I ignore her as I turn to Frankie. "Leo says you know stuff that goes on with the drama group. Did you know Sophia bribed Perrin for the role of Nala?"

"No, and I know it isn't true. She got the role because of her talent." Frankie stands taller than all of us and is so skinny that his loose black clothes hang on him.

"Are you sure?" I ask, confused. "I heard Sonali should have gotten the role."

"Sonali tried out for another role." Frankie's green hat flops as he shakes his head. "I was there for the auditions. After Sophia auditioned, Mrs. Ross stood up and applauded and said that Sophia was perfect for Nala."

Leo taps his chin thoughtfully. "Was Perrin there too?"

"Yeah." Frankie nods. "He's always lurking around."

"Sophia doesn't realize how good she is," Becca adds with a sad sigh. "Even though she's super talented, she's insecure. And now her secret has gone viral and she'll be devastated. I'm going straight to homeroom and talk to her."

"Go ahead," I say with soft sympathy. "I have something to give Leo; then I'll see you in class."

Becca hurries off, and I tell Frankie I need to talk to Leo alone. Before Leo can object, I tug on his arm and move away behind a giant stuffed penguin.

"Here. For the CCSC treasury." I hand Leo the fifty-dollar bill. "I found another lost dog."

"Excellent!" Leo folds the bill precisely in half, then smoothes it neatly with his finger before folding it again. "Where did you find the dog?"

"Behind D-Lite Donuts yesterday after school."

"But the donut shop is closed in the afternoon."

"I didn't know that." I groan. "I'll tell you more at the Skunk Shack."

I leave the storage room, hurrying for my first class. I'm almost there when I plant my palm to my forehead with a "Duh!" I spent so much time talking to Becca by my locker earlier that I didn't open my locker—and I need my science textbook. So I turn on my heels and race back to my locker.

The warning bell rings just as I'm spinning my locker combo.

The metal door swings open and I stare inside.

What's a wooden block doing in my locker?

- Chapter 16 -
Blocked

The brick-sized wooden block is the wintry-brown color of tree bark, and it looks heavy but is surprisingly light. My fingers leave a trail of prints on the shiny surface. It's smooth to touch, as if there's still life whispering from the wood.

Although the block feels solid, there's a hollow sound when I tap it.

Is something hidden inside?

I feel around for a way to open it, but can't find one.

The halls have grown quiet. Shoving the wooden block back into my locker, I race to class. I'm sliding in my chair as the bell rings.

Ms. Grande announces a group project. We split

up, and before I can go with Becca, Chloe tugs her away from me. Becca gives me an apologetic look as she goes off with Chloe. With an uneven number of students in science, guess who has to work alone?

But the project is cool. We're making flubber, just like the gooey glob in the old Disney movie. All it takes is glue, borax, water, and green dye. When we're done, we put our gooey creations in baggies. I wash the green goo off my hands, but it still shimmers from beneath my fingernails. I don't want flubber spilling in my backpack, so I detour to my locker.

Holding my breath, I slowly open my locker, afraid the wooden block will have vanished like my notebook. But I exhale in relief. The block is still on top of my sweater. I toss the bagged flubber beside it, then hurry to my next class.

During second period, I puzzle over the wooden block. Does it have some special meaning? Does it hold a secret? I'm pretty sure Erik left it—just like I'm sure he stole my notebook. How else could he know about Sophia's bribe?

Whose secret will he expose next?

I really need to talk to Erik. He won't be surprised

to see me since he knows that I know that he knows that I know who he really is.

As I walk through the halls during break, I look around for him. He has black hair that pokes up like porcupine quills and he wears neon-purple sneakers. Usually I can hear him before I see him since he carries a basketball around and bounces it as he walks. I think his locker is near the gym, so I detour there, but no luck.

During lunch, instead of going to the Sparkler table, I look around for Erik's porcupine black hair. But he isn't here.

I whirl around and head for the basketball court outside—and grin when I hear the thump of a basketball. And there's Erik with some of his buddies.

I hesitate, suddenly nervous. Watching people is what I'm comfortable with, not confronting a suspect. But Erik is more than a suspect—I know he's guilty. And if I don't stop him, the next post on the Corning Comic website could be about Leo's real age. I cringe as I image a drawing of Leo in diapers with the post: *What's an eleven-year-old doing in middle school?*

A basketball thuds off the backboard and

bounces my way. I rush over to pick it up. "Toss it back," a kid wearing baggy, black jeans shouts.

Swallowing my courage, I walked over to Erik— holding tight to the ball.

"Thanks." Erik reaches for the ball but I step away from him.

"Not so fast, Erik." I drop my voice to a whisper only he can hear. "Or should I call you the Corning Comic?"

His mouth falls open. "How did...I mean...No idea what you're talking about."

"Sure you do."

"Bug off." He rakes his fingers through his prickly hair.

"Would you rather I tell them who you really are?" I point toward the other guys who stare at us curiously, waiting for the ball.

"You don't know anything."

"Don't I?" I drop my voice. "Corning Comic."

His mouth drops open; then he grabs my arm and pulls me away from the basketball court. "What do you want?" he demands.

"My notebook."

"What notebook?" He rubs his forehead.

"You know," I say angrily. "Return my notebook

by the end of school and delete that horrible post about Sophia, or everyone will find out you're the Corning Comic."

"How can I return something I don't have? And I never delete my posts."

"Do you want your buddies to know you posted the blog that got the most popular basketball coach fired?"

"He *was* illegally betting against our team," Erik says.

"Bet your teammates would be more angry with the Corning Comic than their favorite coach." I gesture to the hoop court.

"But I can't delete posts. My site has thousands of fans, and they trust me to be honest with them. They love my cartoons."

"Your cartoon about Sophia was cruel," I retort.

"Not my fault if the truth hurts." He shrugs, then gestures to his buddies who are staring at us. "I don't know anything about your notebook, so leave me alone."

"Then how did you find out about Sophia?"

"I have my sources," he says smugly.

"Who?"

"As if I'd tell you. Like never." He spits on the

ground. "I got a game to finish, so give back my ball."

"Gladly!" I throw the basketball as hard as I can. "Here!"

I may be small, but I learned how to throw a mean ball from Tori and Ann Marie. Erik lunges for the ball, but it smacks his shoulder and he stumbles backwards. The ball slips through his arms.

Do not underestimate a member of the CCSC, I think.

Smiling, I return to the cafeteria.

War has broken out among the Sparklers.

It's a battlefield of glares, and no one is talking.

I almost turn around and go have lunch with Ann Marie and Tori. But Becca looks worried so I sit down beside her. Sophia and Tyla are on opposite sides of the table as if a battle line was drawn down the middle.

What's going on?

Becca nudges me, then whispers, "Sophia won't talk to Tyla."

"Why not?" I whisper back as I plop my sack

lunch on the table.

"Sophia thinks Tyla told the Corning Comic her secret."

Becca turns away from me and reaches across the table to touch Sophia's hand. "Sophia, don't blame Tyla. It's all a big misunderstanding," she says loudly with a pleading look at the other Sparklers.

"No 'miss' about it—I understand exactly," Sophia says with her icy fury aimed at Tyla. "*She* betrayed me."

"I did not!" Tyla argues.

"I confided in you," Sophia sniffles. "And you blabbed to that horrible Corning Comic."

Tyla shakes her head. "But I didn't tell anyone!"

She's telling the truth. I even feel sorry for her.

Becca turns to me and mouths, "Should we tell them?"

"No," I mouth back. Revealing more secrets would only make things worse.

When I stop by my locker, there's still no notebook—but there's evidence that someone broke into my locker again. Only nothing is missing.

My sweater is tossed on top of the wooden block and the flubber bag has fallen, green oozing into a smear on the bottom of my locker. Yuck. I'd planned to take it home to show my parents, but the baggie is ripped and too messy. Careful not to get green goo on my clothes, I pluck it out with two fingers and dump it in the trash.

During my next classes, the hands on the wall clock are so slow that they seem to be moving backwards. All I can think about is getting back to my locker. Erik better return my notebook soon. If he doesn't, the identity of the Corning Comic won't be a mystery. I'll make sure everyone at school knows—starting with my club mates.

When the last bell rings, I race out of my class so fast I forget my backpack and have to go back for it. When I reach my locker, I spin the combination lock too far, then have to start all over again.

When the lock opens, I stare eagerly into my locker and—

No notebook.

The wooden block is still there, but I still can't open it. Becca and Leo would probably have gotten it open in minutes. I keep turning it over in my hands, feeling for a button or lever, but it's just a block of useless wood.

Tossing the block into my backpack, I slam my locker shut, then go to the bike rack to meet my club mates. I'm glad I can finally tell them some of my secrets. They'll be surprised when I tell them who the Corning Comic is, then show them the ransom note and wooden block.

They're both waiting for me at the bike rack.

Leo always looks so serious in a black vest and slacks. He's balancing his gyro-board on its tip and spinning it like a giant top. Becca leans against the bike rack, her arms lifted as she tames her wild black hair into a ponytail. I smile at the pattern on her latest homemade scrunchie: gray and brown like a tortoise carapace.

"Soooo?" Becca asks as I come up and unlock my bike from the rack. "Did you talk to *him*?"

Leo's gyro-board thuds to the ground as he lets go of it to move closer to me. "Him, who?"

"The Corning Comic," I say. "I'm sure he has my notebook."

"You know who he is?" Leo tilts his head in surprise. "That's like the biggest mystery at school."

"And one of *my* secrets. I talked to him and threatened to reveal his identity if he didn't return my notebook by the end of school."

"And?" Becca asks hopefully.

I hold out my empty hands. "Still no notebook."

My sneakers feel heavy as I wheel my bike from the rack.

"Now you can tell us who he is." Becca leans forward eagerly.

I nod, feeling sad but a little relieved to share such a big secret.

Becca and Leo gather close to me, eagerness bright in their gazes.

"And his name is?" Becca asks.

Other kids are heading our way so I whisper, "I'll tell you at the Skunk Shack."

I hop on my bike but Becca moves in front of me, blocking my way.

"Actually...I can't go," she says, frowning.

My fingers strangle my handlebars. "Why not?" I demand.

"Urgent meeting at Chloe's house." Becca flushes with guilt. "Chloe thinks she can convince Sophia and Tyla to talk to each other."

"Maybe I can help," I offer, my anger fading to concern for Sophia. "I'm a Sparkler for a few more days. I'll go with you."

"Ummm...you can't." Becca looks down at the pavement instead of at me. "Chloe says only full members. I hope you don't mind."

I mind, but not about being excluded from the Sparklers. I mind that Becca is choosing them over the CCSC. But I shrug like it's no big deal.

"Whatever," I say. Then I force a cheerful smile and ask Leo, "Want to ride around and look for lost animals? I have the flyers Mom gave me in my backpack."

"Sorry, but I have to cancel too. I'm helping Frankie fix a gear on the warthog." Leo glances over my shoulder, then waves. "Here's Frankie now. I got to go."

Leo hops on his gyro-board and rolls away. When I turn back to Becca, she's pedaling out of the school lot.

I'm disappointed. I'm angry. Mostly, I just feel alone. So I hop on my bike and ride around, looking for lost pets.

We're having unseasonably warm weather for early April, and the sun is like a toaster set on high on my skin. An hour later, I haven't found any lost pets. I'm sweating and thirsty, and my skin is a rosy-pink shade of burned. So I give up and head home.

I'm halfway to the apartment building, paused at an intersection and waiting for a group of kids

with a traffic guard guiding them. Beyond the kids,
a bicyclist rides past.

I blink, recognizing the black bike and rider.

My brother, Kyle.

- Chapter 17 -
Dino Tales

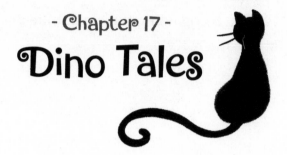

Kyle isn't carrying a box, but he's pedaling like he's on a mission. High school just ended so he should be going home. Instead he's headed downtown.

Where is he going?

"Follow that brother," I say to myself as the street clears. I kick up the speed on my bike and pedal after him.

Like the last time I followed Kyle, he makes a left toward the east side of Sun Flower. I turn left too, staying far enough behind so he won't notice me. He stops at a crosswalk, then again for a stop sign. He even stops at an empty intersection. It's easy to keep him in sight.

He picks up speed though as we approach the

strip mall where I lost him last time. I pick up my speed too. I will *not* lose him again.

As I expected, Kyle turns left into the same shopping center. I speed up when I lose sight of him and make the same left...and he's gone.

Did he duck through the alley?

I slip from sunlight to shadows as I ride between two buildings. It's earlier in the day this time, so I can see enough to avoid a pothole and broken glass near the dumpster. I come out the other side, knowing I can't be more than a minute behind my brother. I peer down a deserted road where a few empty trucks are parked and then in the other direction where fields of wild grass stretch for miles.

No Kyle.

"*No!* Not again!" I stop near a concrete planter of prickly cactuses and thump my fist on my handlebars. Where did he go?

Could he be in one of the businesses?

Doubling back, I lock my bike in a rack near the sheriff's office.

I try there first. Sheriff Fischer isn't there, but his deputy recognizes me and talks to me with an annoying tone like I'm a little kid. He's a tall, skinny guy with more attitude than smarts. Still I believe him when he shakes head and says he hasn't seen my brother.

The pawnshop is a weird place for my brother to go, but I check there anyway. It's nicer than I expected, like a jewelry store with closed glass cases of watches, rings, necklaces, and other jewelry. Becca would like the sparkly rings.

"Can I help you?" a cute girl with black, spiraled hair asks. She's Kyle's age, wearing a tight black skirt with a bejeweled pink jacket and a sheer pink blouse. Her name tag says, "Peony."

"Did you see a brown-haired guy riding a bike come by here?"

"Was he hot-looking?" she asks, dimpling.

"Yuck." I make a gross face. "He's my brother."

She laughs, then gestures around the aisles of glass cases. "As you can see, there aren't any bikes here—and no brothers. But if your brother is cute and single, tell him to stop by and ask for Peony."

I can still hear her laughing as I leave the business.

Doesn't anyone take me seriously? Peony made me feel like a little kid. No way will I tell my brother—or any cute guy—to stop by her store.

Next, I walk by the law office. A large front window gives me a view inside to a cozy waiting area with a comfy couch, a coffee machine, and a table piled neatly with magazines. A middle-aged receptionist with salt-and-pepper hair pulled back from her lined face reminds me of a lioness guarding the entrance to her den.

I take a deep breath to work up some courage, then push open the engraved glass door.

"May I help you?"

If a voice could freeze, I'd now be a human popsicle. The receptionist's black brows narrow together into sharp points. "May I help you, young lady?" she repeats.

"Um...I was looking for...um...my brother." I keep my hand on the door handle, ready for a quick escape.

"And who might he be?" She taps a pen against her desk.

"Um...Kyle. Is he back there?" I look beyond her to a hallway that deepens into shadows dark enough to hide a boy and his bike.

"If he was, due to client confidentially, I wouldn't be allowed to confirm or deny your question."

I take that as a no, then squeak out something that sounds like "thank you." I scurry out the door and down the sidewalk.

I'm ready to jump on my bike and pedal away... until the sweet aroma of pepperoni and pizza sauce entices me. I hear the irresistible catchphrase, "Make history with Prehistoric Pizza."

A costumed dinosaur with a shiny green tail is waving a sign and announcing a special discounted Dino-Roni Bacon Pizza. It's a girl dinosaur and she sounds nice. I can't afford the special or even a slice of pizza, but maybe the dinosaur saw my brother.

"Excuse me," I say, peering into friendly hazel eyes shining from a rubbery dinosaur face. "I'm looking for my brother, Kyle. Did you see a guy go by on a bike?"

"Sorry, but I don't know anyone named Kyle." Her dino tail flops as she shakes her head. "I might have missed him. It's not easy to see much in this costume."

"Oh." My shoulders sag. "Sorry to bother you."

"No bother at all." I can only see hazel eyes through her dinosaur face, but I can tell she's smiling. "I'm bored standing out here alone."

"And I'll bet you're hot in that heavy costume," I say.

"Sizzling! Maybe I can help you." She points to the front of the Prehistoric Pizza. "With all those windows, my coworkers might have seen your brother. I was just getting ready to take a short break. While I'm inside, I'll ask Gina, Steve, K. C., and Reynaldo. But I won't ask the manager, Mr. Kinkaid—he's meaner than a T. rex. What does your brother look like?"

"Tall, thin with brown hair."

"That could be a lot of guys. But I'll check. Wait here." She goes inside, and I tap my sneaker on the pavement, counting the taps until I get over two hundred and lose count. I'm up to seventy-three again when she returns.

"Sorry." She shakes her dinosaur head. "No Kyle inside."

"Drats," I say with heavy disappointment.

"You look thirsty so I brought you an orange soda." She holds out a plastic cup. "By the way, I'm Talla."

"I'm Kelsey, and thank you." I sip bubbly orange sweetness. "Getting this soda is the best thing that's happened today."

"Not a great day?" Talla asks sympathetically.

I grimace. "The worst!"

"At least you're not stuck in a hot costume," she complains. "I'm glad my shift is almost over. I'm sweating like I'm wearing a sleeping bag on the hottest day of summer."

"So why work here?" I ask, then take another sip.

She laughs. "Who wouldn't want to get paid to be a dinosaur?"

I nod, understanding. When I was little, I loved everything about dinosaurs and could pronounce even the longest, most complicated names.

"Thanks again," I say, gesturing to the drink. "I better go."

"Sorry I couldn't help find your brother."

"He has a way of just vanishing." I smile wryly. "At least I know where he didn't go—not the sheriff, the pawnshop, or the pizza place."

"What about the law office?" Her tail flops with a thump as she turns to point to the remaining business.

"I hope he's not there because I never want to talk to that Ice Queen receptionist again." I shiver. "Besides, Kyle doesn't need a lawyer."

"Are you sure?" she asks. "The description of your brother matches this guy I've recognized from my high school—I don't know his name—who's gone to the law office at least three times this week."

"What high school?" My siblings all go to Sun Flower High, but some kids go to a private school, Creative Minds Academy.

"Sun Flower High," Talla says.

"Did he ride a black bike?" I ask uneasily.

"I didn't notice." She shrugs her dino shoulders. "All I know is that I've seen him at school hanging with some basketball players so he's probably a jock."

Before my family lost their home and Kyle got obsessed with scholarship applications, he was on a basketball team.

But why would my brother need a lawyer?

- Chapter 18 -
Tortoise Trouble

Kyle doesn't come home for dinner that night.

"He's with Jake," Mom says cheerfully. "I'm so glad he's finally getting out. It's wonderful he's seeing his friends again."

It would be if that were true.

And I shudder at the memory of the scary law-office receptionist.

My brain is on overload and it's hard to go to sleep. I lie in bed, staring up at my ceiling where slivers of moonlight shift into puzzle pieces that don't connect.

Kyle + Lawyer = Trouble.

I think of all the reasons someone might need a lawyer, but most of my ideas come from TV crime dramas. I'm pretty sure Kyle isn't guilty of murder, kidnapping, grand larceny, identity theft, or assault with a deadly weapon. If it were illegal to get obsessed over applying for colleges, Kyle would be guilty.

I fall asleep with images of Kyle riding his bicycle with a box that ticks like a bomb...

The next day at school I wait for Becca by my locker, but she doesn't show up. Will she bother coming to the Skunk Shack for our CCSC meeting after school? Both Becca and Leo have been so busy lately that I feel like I'm in a club of one.

I find Becca in our homeroom, her dark ponytail sweeping across Chloe's desk while they whisper. As I walk down the aisle, I frown at Sophia's empty chair. Is she ever coming back to school?

Sitting behind Becca, I wait for her to turn around but she's too busy talking to Chloe. I thump my science book on my desk.

Becca whirls to face me. "Oh, Kelsey. You're here."

"I waited for you by my locker." I try not to sound whiny.

"I had to talk with Chloe." She drops her voice so only I can hear. "We went to Sophia's house last night, and she's a mess. She won't get out of bed and is faking sick to skip school. She thinks everyone hates her. That horrible Corning Comic destroyed her confidence."

"I can destroy him," I say carefully. "Want to know his name?"

"Of course I do!" Her bracelets, silver like her Sparkler necklace, jangle as she gestures excitedly.

"It's Er—"

"Becca!" Chloe calls out. "I just thought of a new plan to help Sophia."

With a shrug, Becca mouths, "Tell me at lunch," and turns back to Chloe. They start whispering again.

But Becca walks into the lunchroom with Chloe, so there's no chance to talk to her alone. When the lunch bell rings and we leave the cafeteria, Becca pulls me toward her and whispers into my ear, "We'll talk about the Corning Comic at our CCSC meeting. Afterward we can stop by my house to cuddle with our kittens, then bike around searching for lost pets."

I feel a little better and smile. "Sounds like a plan."

"Exactly! See you then." With a hand wave, Becca hurries to her next class.

After school, Becca is waiting for me by the bike rack and Leo is with her. I walk with a skip in my step. The CCSC is together again. My club mates will be so surprised when I show them the ransom note and the wooden block.

"Race you to the Skunk Shack," I throw out as a challenge while I unlock my bike from the rack.

"Um...I'm not going." Leo frowns, and I notice he's not carrying his gyro-board. "That's what I came to tell you."

"If you say you *have* to help Frankie again, I'll scream," I warn through gritted teeth.

"Don't scream! I hate loud noises." Leo looks panicked.

"What do you care what I do? You'd rather be with Frankie than us."

"The play's dress rehearsal is soon. Frankie needs my help."

"And of course only *you* can help him," I spat back. "Well, your club needs you too!" I turn to Becca for support. "Tell him we're sick of being ditched for Frankie all the time."

"Well...I would but—"

"Becca, do *not* say you can't come either," I warn through clenched teeth.

"I'll be there—just a little late." Becca twists her ponytail around her finger, her gaze drifting across a grassy lawn to the street where two girls stand with their bikes: Chloe and Tyla.

"You're going with *them!*" My hand shakes with anger as I point to the other two Sparkler girls.

"It won't take long," Becca cries. "Sophia refuses to talk to Tyla or help at the fund-raiser and may even quit the play. We're having an intervention at her house."

"I guess I'm not invited to this either?" I snap.

"I'm sorry but they..." Becca spreads out her arms helplessly. "Tyla only wants me and Chloe. We won't take long, and then I'll hurry to the Skunk Shack."

"What's the point? We can't have a meeting without our covert technology strategist," I say, giving Leo a furious look.

"I could make more meetings if Frankie was a member," Leo says. "Frankie would be an asset to the CCSC. He can create superior disguises that are much more effective than a hat or wig."

"My disguises work fine," I argue.

"Only at a distance. Frankie has turned actors into cats, robots, historical people, and more. It's only logical to invite him into the CCSC. I even have a title for him: disguise expert."

I fold my arms across my chest. "We'll vote on Frankie at our next meeting."

"Will you vote yes?" Leo tilts his head toward me.

Instead of answering, I shoot him a suspicious look. "Have you been avoiding our meetings because I won't vote the way you want?"

"That behavior would be childish, and I have never been childish. Not even when I was a child." Leo looks down at his vest, smoothing a crease.

"But is it true?" I persist.

"According to my calculations, there's only a 32 percent chance you'll say yes. By giving you time to get to know Frankie, the odds improve to 48 percent."

Becca gasps. "You've been skipping our meetings on purpose?"

"While that would be a logical strategy, I have been truthful about helping Frankie." Leo looks hopefully at me. "Will you vote for him?"

I shift my heavy backpack on my back as I consider my answer. I like Frankie, but something about him makes me uneasy.

"My vote is still no," I tell Leo. "Our club is perfect with just the three of us. We've solved three mysteries and get along great—at least when we work together."

"You won't change your mind?" When I shake my head, Leo's shoulders sag and he walks away without even saying good-bye.

I feel guilty. But I won't change my vote.

I roll my bike from the rack and swing my leg over to sit on my seat. "Becca, I'll see you at the Skunk Shack."

"Since you'll get there before me, could you go check on Albert? Mom says he hasn't been eating and she's worried about him."

"He misses Reggie," I guess with a sigh. "Sure, I'll check on him."

"Thanks. Albert has to start eating soon, or Mom will give him away. And since you're going to check on Albert, could you try to feed him too? There are carrots in the fridge for him. If he eats, Mom won't be in such a hurry to find him a new home."

I nod, willing to do anything to help Albert.

I kick off my bike and ride alone to Wild Oaks Sanctuary.

Since I'm going to Becca's house first, I pass by

the gated back entrance that trails through thick brush to the Skunk Shack. Riding under the arched front entrance into Wild Oaks, I wind down the graveled driveway to Becca's ranch-style home.

Mrs. Morales welcomes me with a hug. "It's wonderful to see you, Kelsey. But where's Becca?"

Good question, I think bitterly.

"She's helping a friend but will be here soon. She asked me to feed Albert."

"If you can get Albert to eat, that would be amazing!"

Mrs. Morales goes into the kitchen, two ferrets on her heels. Becca calls them the Fur Bros. I hear a mew and look down to see a whirl of orange. Bending down, I scoop Honey into my arms. She purrs and rubs her furry head against me. She's so sweet, and I wish so much I could bring her home.

When Becca's kitten, Chris, scampers by, Honey wiggles out of my arms and bounds after him.

"Here's a fresh bunch of carrots," Mrs. Morales says when she returns holding carrots that have a rough, natural look like they were just plucked from the ground. "Take these to Albert."

"Thanks," I say, reaching out.

"I hope you can get that big fellow to eat,"

Mrs. Morales says as she follows me to the door. "I've been on the phone with Abigail DeSesa from the CTTC—the California Turtle & Tortoise Club— and she says it's common for tortoises to bond with their owners and get depressed when they're gone. I've tried all kinds of foods to tempt Albert, but he won't eat."

"I'll do my best," I promise.

Albert doesn't even lift his wrinkly neck when I come up to him and wave a carrot. He looks the same to me...but different. His eyes don't shine as brightly. And he ignores the carrot, even when I put it up to his mouth.

"Oh, Albert," I whisper, finding a rock that's not splattered with bird poo to sit on. "Please, eat something."

He sinks into his shell until all I can see is the top of his head.

"You miss Reggie," I say softly. "You're sad because you're lonely. Well, I'll tell you a secret...I feel lonely too."

Albert doesn't move but I know he's listening.

"My friends are cool most of the time." I suck in a deep breath, then blow it out. "But lately they're always going off with other friends and leaving me behind. Becca says I'm a Sparkler—at least until the fund-raiser on Saturday—but the Sparklers only include me when they want my help. And Leo would rather hang out with Frankie."

Albert stretches his neck and looks at me.

"Being alone sucks," I say.

The tortoise bobs his head.

"Yeah, I understand. I want to be with Becca and Leo, and you want to be with Reggie."

We sit awhile in silence: thirteen-year-old girl and hundred-thirty-year-old tortoise. Different species yet we have something in common: we both miss our friends.

I keep trying to convince Albert to eat. He won't even look at me, so I come up with an idea. I lift one of the raw carrots and spin it like a baton in my fingers. He still isn't interested, so I bring the carrot to my mouth and take a big crunchy bite.

"Albert, try the yummy carrots," I say through chews.

His black eyes watch the carrot. I take another bite, then hold out the carrot. He stretches his wrinkly neck and sniffs. Finally! He's going to eat!

Only he droops his head and withdraws under his shell.

The carrots hang heavy in my hand as I turn away.

A short time later, I'm on my way to the Skunk Shack. As I near the tree-shrouded building, I hear laughter coming from inside. I park my bike by the large table-sized stump, then hurry into the shack.

Leo and Becca sit at the lopsided table, sipping juice drinks with a few papers spread out between them.

My brows rise with surprise. "What are you doing here?"

"A rather obvious question," Leo says. "We're waiting for you so we can start our CCSC meeting."

"But I didn't think you were coming."

"I was surprised to see Leo too," Becca admits. "And pleased."

Leo lifts his stylus from his tablet, then taps it on the table like a gavel. "I hereby call our CCSC meeting to order."

"I second that," Becca says cheerfully.

They turn to me and I'm so happy we're all here that I can't stop smiling. The CCSC is back together.

"I third the motion," I say as I sit beside them at the table.

Once Leo gets past his treasurer's report and other boring topics, I announce that I have *news* to share.

I unzip my backpack and hold out the wooden block and the ransom note.

"Is this another spy game challenge?" Becca asks.

"No," I say, remembering the challenges I gave them when we first formed the club. Becca pieced together a ripped spy message, and Leo escaped from locked handcuffs.

"Not a game—the real thing." I explain how I found both in my locker.

"So the ransom note led you to that missing dog you found?" Leo asks, wrinkling his brow so deeply he reminds me a little of Albert.

"It was great finding the dog, but I still don't have my notebook." I point to the wooden block. "And now all I have is *this*—whatever it is."

"It appears to be a Japanese puzzle box." Leo turns it over in his hands. "Usually I can open them quickly by moving sliding panels."

"I don't see any panels." I crane my neck forward to watch as Leo runs his fingers over the smooth wood.

Leo frowns. "The level of difficulty is high."

"Let me try," Becca says.

"While other toddlers stacked toy blocks, I assembled Lego robotics and solved complex puzzles," he says in his annoying superior tone. "Ah! I found a crevice...Apply pressure here and push this tiny wood panel, then—"

Click.

A popsicle-stick-like wood slat pops up, revealing a secret compartment.

When Leo flips the box over and shakes it, a strip of paper—like you find in a fortune cookie—flutters out.

I catch the paper.

And read.

- Chapter 19 -
Cryptic Clue

At least, I *try* to read the message.

"It starts off with *W-E*, but then the rest is jumbled letters and numbers that don't make any sense," I say, wrinkling my brow.

"They could form acronyms," Leo guesses. "Each letter represents a word."

"Like CCSC." Becca smiles. "Or maybe it's another language."

Leo shakes his blond head. "Not any language I know."

I snap my fingers. "Spy language!"

"There is no such thing." Leo scoffs.

"Spies communicate in code. I've studied common codes that spies use. Some are so complex that only a computer can solve them."

"Let's go to my house and decipher the code on my computer," Leo says.

"Not necessary." I stare down at the tiny print, recognizing a familiar pattern. "I can figure it out. It's an easy letter-substitution code."

"A cryptogram," Leo says with a nod. "I prefer sudoku puzzles, but I've solved many cryptograms."

I take the paper over to the table and smooth it out.

WE MJP GQLS SJ EWLB MJPA NZUAZSN,

IJJV WL IJUVZA 299

"Is it weird to have numbers mixed in with letters?" Becca scoots in beside me and points to the paper.

"Not weird at all," I say, then take out paper and a pencil from my backpack. I copy the code down in large print, then write the alphabet across the top of the page.

While I prefer to figure things out on paper, Leo consults his tablet.

"Each letter represents another letter," I explain to Becca while I scan the paper in search of a starting place.

"Or it could be more complicated where you

have to count down from each corresponding letter to match the code with the correct letter," Leo says.

"Huh?" Becca blinks at him.

Leave it to Leo to make something simple sound like advanced algebra. While Leo taps away on his device, I explain to Becca, "Becca, see these two *J*s together?"

She nods.

"That means it's a double vowel or consonant. And the most commonly doubled letters are *d*, *e*, *f*, *g*, *l*, *m*, *n*, *o*...Oh, I think I know!" I write the letter *O* beneath the letter *J* on my alphabet list. "It's the word 'look!'"

Leo stops mid-keystroke to look at me. "You can't possibly know the word from a wild guess."

"But it's not a guess." I tap my pencil on the paper. "This puzzle probably came from the person who stole my notebook and left the ransom note. The first word of the ransom note was *look* so it's logical to find that word here too."

"Good deduction." Leo approves. "That means *I* is *L* and *V* is *K*."

"The last word begins with *L-O*...and then there's the number."

"Locker 299!" Becca guesses.

After that, other words fall into place. *SJ* is a small word ending with *O*. Easy to guess it's *to*, a very common small word.

So when we're finished, the decoded message reads:

If you want to find your secrets, look in locker 299.

"What are we waiting for?" I jump up and grab my backpack.

"School's been over for hours." Leo frowns. "The gates will be locked. We'll have to wait till the morning."

"I can't wait," I say with a stubborn shake of my head. "I have to find the notebook."

"If we can't get in through the gates, we'll find another way," Becca says.

We lock up the Skunk Shack, then head to Helen Corning Middle School. Becca and I ride our bikes while Leo hops on his gyro-board.

All during the ride, I'm thinking of Locker 299, excited and scared of what I'll find. Will there be another puzzle to solve? Will I finally get my notebook back? Or will there be nothing at all?

But I wonder why the thief—especially if it's Erik—would bother to leave cryptic clues when he didn't even want to talk to me yesterday. And he didn't seem worried when I threatened to expose his identity—which I haven't done yet. But I will if Locker 299 doesn't hold my notebook.

It made sense for him to want my notebook. With nearly forty entries, the notebook gives him weeks of dramatic secrets to post. His web hits will soar to insane numbers, and people I care about will be hurt. Words are explosive weapons, striking deep into heart and soul.

But wait a minute...how can it be Erik? I found the wooden box in my locker *before* I threatened to expose him if he didn't return the notebook. How is that possible?

I'll figure it out later—once I have my notebook back.

When we reach the school, one of our fears is confirmed.

While the athletic fields are open for the public, the school buildings are padlocked for the night. There's no way to get to the lockers—unless we break in. I have my key-spider lock pick, but I won't break into my own school.

"Drats." I coast my bike between Leo's gyro-board and Becca's bike. "I don't want to wait until tomorrow."

"You won't wait a full day," Leo points out. "According to my calculations, the school opens in only 15.3 hours."

"There may be a way inside." Becca shields her eyes from the setting sun and peers off to the back field where baseball, soccer, and other sports are played. In the distance I hear the rumble of a lawn mower again.

"How?" I ask.

"A smile is more effective than a key." Becca whirls her bike around and pedals down a side road.

Leo and I look at each other, shrug, and then hurry to catch up with her.

The rumble of the lawn mower grows louder, and I recognize our groundskeeper, Mr. Thompson, riding it. Not far away, some kids practice baseball. I can't even guess what Becca is planning until she parks her bike on the sidewalk, then runs over to Mr. Thompson.

"What is she doing?" Leo asks, stopping his gyro-board beside Becca's bike.

I shake my head. "I don't know. But she's waving

at Mr. Thompson."

"He turned off the mower," Leo says with a puzzled tilt of his head. "Should we go over there?"

"I don't think she needs our help." I stare as Becca's smile widens while she talks to Mr. Thompson. I can't see his expression beneath his thick, black beard, but he's nodding and stepping off his mower.

"They're coming this way!" Leo says.

Becca leads the groundskeeper over to our bikes. He smells of sweet grass as he tips back his cap to smile at us. "So I hear you have a problem," he says in a gruff, kindly voice like he really is Hagrid come to life.

"Um...yeah, I guess we do," I say with a questioning look at Becca.

"Not to worry," Mr. Thompson says, and I notice the expensive watch on his tanned arm. He may not brag about his reality-show win, but that watch isn't from a discount store.

"Mr. Thompson volunteers at Wild Oaks, weeding and gardening," Becca explains to us.

"I believe in giving back to my community," the groundskeeper says modestly. "Your mother is doing so much to help animals."

"She works hard," Becca admits. "But she couldn't do it without all the volunteers and donations."

Mr. Thompson nods, and I suspect he's also one of the people who donate.

"Always glad to help for a good cause." He has a huge bunch of keys to every lock at the school, and he sorts through them now until he holds up a shining silver key. "I'm not just groundskeeper—I also do some of the custodian work. I'll wait here while you run to your locker. Be quick, since I'm bending the rules."

He leads us to the back school gate. Becca and I park our bikes, while Leo taps the remote for his gyro-board so that it follows behind him like an obedient puppy. Mr. Thompson's keys jangle as he opens the gate for us.

Feeling Mr. Thompson's gaze on my back, I turn to Becca. "Does he know that it isn't *our* locker?"

"I told him the truth," Becca says simply.

"Which version of the truth?" I ask.

"I said it's urgent that I get into Locker 299." She slowly smiles. "I can't help it if he thinks it's *my* locker."

"We'll find out who owns it soon." Leo points to a bank of lockers near the gym.

"I have my key spider with me," I add, patting my backpack. "Although I don't think it'll open a combination lock."

Locker 299 is the last locker in the top row, scratched and battered like ballplayers used it for target practice.

I pull out my key spider, but Leo waves it away and presses his ear near the combination dial. "I've studied how to crack combination locks. You just listen for the tumblers to click."

"Or you reach out and open the door." I point. "The lock is broken."

I nudge Leo aside and tug on the door handle. As I pull on it, the door falls open.

Holding my breath, I look inside...

- Chapter 20 -
Sweet Celebration

"It's here!" I reach into the locker and hug my precious secret-filled notebook.

"*Fantastique!*" Becca comes over to peer inside the locker. "Nothing else inside. I was hoping for another clue or a written confession from the thief."

"I have my notebook back!" I hug it like a mother reunited with a lost child. "It's like a miracle."

"According to my calculations, there was a 61 percent chance the notebook would be recovered," Leo says. "I expected it to be here."

I'm too happy to be annoyed by Mr. Know-It-All. I caress the smooth green cover of my notebook. I'll never, ever take it to school again. The secrets will stay safe in my hidden drawer and will never leave my room.

Of course this doesn't mean the secrets are still secret. The thief probably read them and copied the pages. If it's Erik, I know his secret so he won't reveal any more of mine. But what if someone else is guilty?

When we return to the gate, Becca flashes her sweetest smile at Mr. Thompson. "Thanks so much!" she tells him.

"Found what you needed?" the burly grounds-keeper asks.

"Oh yes!" I say, still hugging my notebook.

"You've been so kind and we're really grateful," Becca adds.

"Glad to help out." Mr. Thompson's massive key ring jangles as he locks the gate behind us. "Now I've got mowing to finish. Have a great day, kids."

I flip through my notebook. "I'm so glad I have it back. And it's in good shape. No rips or missing pages."

Becca grins. "Another mystery solved by the CCSC!"

"Our combined skills make us a great team," Leo says.

"We haven't been much of a team lately," I say,

hurt feelings rushing up to catch in my throat. I glance down at my sneakers, noticing a blade of grass on my left toe. I reach down to brush it off, then glance uneasily at my friends.

Leo knits his brows at me. "The CCSC is *very* important to me."

"Is something wrong, Kelsey?" Becca studies me. "I thought you'd be happy you got your notebook back."

"Yeah...I am but you've both been busy with other friends so much lately that it's like I'm in our club alone." I suck in a deep breath, not wanting to complain, but holding my real feelings inside would be dishonest, like lying. So I dig deep and spit it all out. "My feelings are hurt...Like you don't care about our club—or me—anymore."

"You can't be serious." Leo tilts his head as if trying to figure me out. "I had no idea you felt that way. I'll admit I don't always pick up on social cues and I enjoy helping Frankie out. But I didn't mean to hurt your feelings."

"Me neither." Becca reaches over to squeeze my hand. "Don't feel left out. Didn't I invite you to join the Sparklers?"

"Temporarily." I twist the Sparkler necklace

between my fingers, the light chain surprisingly heavy on my neck. "I don't care about the Sparklers, but the CCSC means a lot to me. Belonging to a club of friends who work to help animals makes me feel like I'm doing something important."

"And it's fun," Becca adds. Then she leans in to whisper, "Here's a secret for your notebook: I care more about our club than the Sparklers."

A heavy weight inside me lightens and I realize I'm smiling.

"I apologize if I've injured your feelings," Leo says with such a confused expression that I feel sorry for him. "I didn't know you felt left out. We can keep the club the same just like you want. We don't need to add any new members."

He sounds so sad that I feel a little guilty. But I don't want Frankie in our club so I nod. "Our club has been really successful," I say in a more cheerful tone. "We've solved mysteries and reunited pets with their owners. And we even donated half of our reward money to the Humane Society. I vote we celebrate our success. Do I hear a second?"

"Second," Leo says, raising his hand.

"And third. But can we wait till tomorrow?" Becca asks. "I promised Mom to help with the animals."

"Sure. After school, let's celebrate the Case family way." I straddle my bike, then turn back to my friends with a big grin. "A cookie-making party at my house."

"Irresistible invitation." Leo smacks his lips together. "I'll be there."

"I never say no to cookies," Becca says. "Eating or making them."

We curve our fingers into a *C*, bump knuckles, and air-shape the letter *S*, then kick off and ride away.

As I pedal home, I'm thinking about the CCSC and smiling.

It's strange how a few hours can change everything. I don't feel alone anymore. I have my green notebook. And my club mates and I are going to have a delicious cookie celebration.

Sure, there are still troubling questions: Is Erik the notebook thief? How can we get Albert to eat? And where does my brother go when he vanishes?

I don't expect to hear from Becca until tomorrow, so I'm surprised when I'm getting ready for bed that night and Mom comes into my room with the phone. I wait till Mom leaves the room, then ask, "What's up, Becca?"

"Kelsey!" She squeals so loudly that I pull the phone away from my ears. "You'll never guess what I found out!"

"What?" I sink down on the edge of my bed to brace myself.

"I just checked the Corning Comic's website," she says breathlessly.

"Did he post more of my secrets?" I tense and grip the phone tight.

"The opposite—all the cartoons are gone. The website has been shut down."

"But why?" I switch the phone to my other ear as I walk over to my window and stare into darkness. "I asked him to delete the post about Sophia—not his whole site."

"You really scared him. Way to go, Kelsey. You used your superpower wisely."

Something doesn't add up but I'm thrilled the site is down. I rake my fingers through my hair. "I guess this means he stole my notebook."

"Sophia will be so happy. I'm going to call her now and convince her to come back to school and not quit the play."

"Good luck," I say, but I'm more confused than ever as I hang up the phone.

Before I go to sleep, I take my notebook from my backpack. I stare down at the green cover with *Notebook of Secrets* black-inked across the top. Writing down secrets is fun and makes me feel like Harriet the Spy 2. But it would have been horrible for my family and friends if the secrets were exposed.

So I have to quit.

No more collecting secrets.

Kneeling in front of my wooden chest, I slide the book inside. The hidden drawer closes with a soft thud. And I vow never to open it again.

The next morning, Becca isn't waiting for me at my locker, but Leo is there with an excited expression as he waves a printout.

"I have information on Reggie," Leo announces with the enthusiasm of a TV game-show host. He kind of looks the role too, in a shiny black vest over a starchy white shirt and formal black slacks.

"Did you talk to Reggie?" I ask eagerly.

"No—but thanks to Frankie, we'll have his phone number soon."

Frankie again, I think. Frowning, I turn to my locker and grab my science book.

I slam my locker door shut and turn back to Leo. "Great work," I say.

"Actually Frankie did all the detective work," Leo explains. "Working in the drama club, he knows a lot about actors and says professional actors usually have an agent. He found the phone number for Reggie's agent, Emily Shaw."

"That's great! Did you call her?"

Leo shakes his head. "Conversing with informants is a job for our social operative so I gave Becca the number."

"Did I hear my name?" Becca asks, coming into our conversation. She looks chic in a tie-dyed wrap dress with a knotted front and a rainbow ribbon woven in her black ponytail. "Are you having a club meeting without me?"

Leo furrows his brow indignantly. "This is clearly *not* a club meeting. Our meetings are only held in the Skunk Shack."

"Becca was just joking." I chuckle.

"But it wasn't funny like a pun or a knock-knock joke."

"Not all jokes are actually jokes," I try to explain,

but I can tell by Leo's puzzled expression that he doesn't get it. Shrugging, I turn to Becca. "Leo was just telling me about finding Reggie's agent. Did you call her?"

"Not yet." Becca pushes a loose black curl from her face. "It's too early so I'll wait till later. Poor Albert misses Reggie so much. The sweet shelled baby is moping around and still won't eat."

"Albert could die without Reggie," I say with a heavy heart.

"Once Reggie is aware of the situation, he will return," Leo says confidently. "According to my calculations, assuming he finds out about Albert today and factoring in the speed of travel by car, Reggie will be back Saturday evening."

But will that be soon enough for Albert?

I fall into step with Becca as we head for class through the crowded halls. Overhead lights flash on Becca's silver crescent moon necklace, and I touch the identical necklace I'm wearing. After the fund-raiser tomorrow, I'll return the necklace. My temporary Sparkler status will be over. And to be honest, I'm relieved.

Becca is the only one at the Sparkler table. I glance around and see Tyla and Chloe waiting in the fast food line. Sophia is absent again—probably still too upset to return to school. Dumping my backpack on the floor, I sit beside Becca.

She leans close to whisper, "I talked to the agent! I was super nervous because a Hollywood type with famous friends might not even talk to a kid. But she didn't hang up on me!"

"Did she tell you Reggie's number?"

"She said she can't divulge client info." Becca rips into a bag of chips. I'm surprised but pleased that she's brown-bagging her lunch like me. "But after I explained about Albert, she was really sympathetic because she had a desert tortoise when she was little. She said Reggie was filming in a remote location, but she'd contact him and ask him to call me."

"The sooner, the better for Albert." I open my brown bag and unwrap a triple-layered honey ham sandwich on banana nut bread. "Now we just wait."

"My phone is on vibrate so I don't miss his call." Becca pats her backpack.

We talk about Albert for a while. Becca saw him drinking water, but otherwise he hides in his shell.

"Speaking of tortoise shells—look what I've designed," Becca says in a brighter tone and holds out a square of cotton fabric. "Does it look like a tortoise carapace?"

The fabric is fawn brown blended with a shimmering gray. "It's gorgeous," I say.

"I'm sewing a club vest for each of us," she says excitedly.

"A club outfit." I smile. "I love it."

"Love what?" Tyla interrupts in the chilly tone she uses just for me. Chloe follows behind her, and they sit down across from us.

"Kelsey was admiring my new design." Becca waves the square of fabric.

"Why are you wasting time with that instead of creating face-painting designs?" Tyla says with a disapproving sniff. "That's what I spent hours doing last night."

Tyla plops her large sketch pad between the lunch trays, and then Becca and Chloe spend the rest of lunch admiring Tyla's drawings. I sneak peeks too, although I pretend not to care. I have to admit that she's very talented. Her mermaids look magical with hair spilling like ocean waves, and her unicorns seem to fly and leap off the page.

"Each unicorn has a crescent star necklace," Tyla says with a dramatic finger snap. "Just like a Sparkler!"

I tune out Tyla and think of cookies.

When I told my parents I wanted to have a cookie celebration, they loved the idea. Chef Dad was the most enthusiastic. He offered to have ingredients ready to make his most popular cookie creation: ChipTastics. These jumbo cookies are a sweet and salty combination of nuts, chips, and candy pieces. I don't know what the secret ingredient is because Dad won't reveal that recipe to anyone.

We'll have the kitchen to ourselves, although Dad will be close by if we need help. Mom said she'd read in her room. My sisters will be at a school dance. And my brother? He says he's going "out" — whatever that means.

I hope he doesn't end up in jail.

When school ends, I race to meet Becca as she leaves her last class.

"No call from Reggie," Becca says before I can even ask.

"Drats." We fall in step, weaving through throngs of kids. Fridays are always a little crazy with everyone hurrying to escape school for the weekend — even teachers.

We're not meeting at the Skunk Shack because

Becca has to do chores before she can come to my house.

"Leo texted that he's tweaking FRODO, but he'll be on time for the cookie celebration," Becca adds.

"He's not with Frankie?" I ask, surprised.

Becca shrugs. "Guess not."

It's strange to be home so early on a school day, but kind of nice. I lounge on my bed and pick up where I left off in *Harriet the Spy*. Harriet's friends won't talk to her because they read her notebook, and I wish I could tell her to tell them the truth. A spy doesn't have to reveal all of her secrets, but she needs to be honest with her friends.

After dinner and dish-washing duty, Dad shoos me out of kitchen. "I'll get everything ready for your cookie celebration."

Pans clang and cupboards creak open, then bang shut while I wait in the living room. The TV blares a sitcom but I'm not paying attention. I keep glancing at the wall clock, counting seconds.

When the doorbell rings, I jump up. I race for the door, but Mom gets there first and invites Becca and Leo into our apartment.

Mom goes to her room while I lead Becca and Leo into the kitchen.

"Voilà!" Dad says with a dramatic flourish of his hands toward the kitchen island, which is arranged with cookie sheets, a mixing bowl, measuring cups, and plastic containers of sugar, flour, and other ingredients.

"Since this is your celebration," Dad says with a twinkle in his eyes, "I've mixed the dry ingredients—including a few secret spices—but left the rest for you. Be sure to grease and flour the cooking trays. Here are the printed instructions." He hands me a paper. "I'll be in the living room watching *The Laughing Chef*. Come get me if you have any questions."

"One question, sir," Leo says with a polite raise of his hand. "Are we measuring in the metric system?"

Dad chuckles. "Let's stick to the U.S. style of quarts, teaspoons, and tablespoons."

"What kind of cookies are we making?" Becca asks.

"ChipTastics—my most popular cookie. They have everything in them! Yogurt chips, chocolate chips, toffee chips, raisins, walnuts, almonds... and a few mysterious spices," Dad says proudly. "Don't worry if you make a mess—that's part of the process. You can clean it up afterward. Have fun."

Fun is very, very messy.

I point and laugh at Becca's flour-splattered cheek. She pretends to be mad and throws flour at me, which goes up my nose. I sneeze, then grab a fistful of flour and hurl it at Becca. She ducks— and flour splatters Leo. He shakes off the flour, then reels back and throws two handfuls at both of us.

Laughing and sputtering, we look like flour-dusted ghosts. But we settle down, wash up, and get busy baking cookies.

We make more cookies than three kids could ever eat. And we only burn one tray of cookies—leaving an acrid odor blending with sugary sweetness.

I'm slipping on an oven mitt to ease the hot tray from the oven when I hear a burst of music. Becca changes her ringtone frequently, and her current melody is from an Ariana Grande song.

Becca wipes her chocolate-smeared fingerprints on a towel, then grabs her phone from the counter. "Hey, Chloe," she says; then she goes quiet.

She's quiet while she listens, her cheerful expression darkening like an eclipse of the sun. "Are you sure? But she can't do that!"

Who can't do what? I wonder.

"Nooooo!" Becca cries like a moan. "We can't survive without her help!"

"What's wrong?" I rush over to Becca, Leo's footsteps padding behind me.

Becca shakes her head, staring down at the phone screen even though it's gone black. She slips the phone into her pocket, then turns toward us.

"Tell us," I say anxiously. "What did Chloe say?"

"It's a disaster." Becca shakes her flour-sprinkled dark head. "Sophia and Tyla had a huge fight."

"Is that all?" I say with some relief. "They argue all the time."

"Not like this."

"At least they're talking now," I point out.

"But they're saying terrible things to each other. Sophia still thinks Tyla told the Corning Comic about the bribe. Tyla called her a liar, and it got worse from there." Becca brushes flour from her ponytail, then tosses her ponytail over her shoulder. "Tyla and Sophia are at war. Even if we tell them the Corning Comic found out because he read your secrets, they'll still hate each other."

"You can tell them if you want." I give her shoulder an encouraging pat. "But they have to solve their own problems."

"Their problem *is* my problem." Becca folds her arms to her chest. "And it's yours too."

I frown. "Why?"

"Tyla refuses to help out at the fund-raiser because Sophia might be there. And Sophia says she won't come because Tyla might be there. Now neither of them will be there. So it'll be just you, me, and Chloe." Becca sags against the kitchen island. "Chloe will pick up the face paints from Tyla, but she can't paint faces."

"I can't either." My hearts sinks.

"And I can't do it alone." Becca moans. "Our booth is going to lose money—not make it. This is the worse thing ever."

I agree with her...but we're both wrong.

When Becca's phone rings again, things get much worse.

- Chapter 21 -
ChipTastic

"It's Mom," Becca says as she turns away to talk in the phone. She just nods, listening until her shoulders go rigid, and she gasps, "Albert!"

When she hangs up, I grip her arm. "Has something happened to Albert?"

"Nothing yet, but it's going to." Becca grimaces.

"What?" Leo and I ask.

"The lady from the tortoise club—Abigail—has found a home for Albert." Becca scowls. "Mom is thrilled. She says it's a great solution."

"No!" The kitchen smells sweet with cookies, but there's a bitter taste in my mouth. "She can't give Albert away."

"She says it's the only way to get him the best

care. His new home will be in Valencia—over 350 miles south—with someone named Tortoise Tom who rescues tortoises. Mom says he's excited to get such an old Aldabra and is already preparing an enclosure for him with a pond and heated building. It's the perfect place for Albert—" Her voice breaks and she sinks down into a kitchen chair.

I come over and put my arm around her.

"Maybe it's for the best," I say. "We don't even know if Reggie will come back. If he got the big acting role, then he has to stay in LA."

"He'll come back," Leo says stubbornly. "Reggie wouldn't abandon Albert."

"Then why hasn't he called?" I argue.

"Kelsey's right." Becca sniffles. "We can't count on Reggie to take Albert back. He abandoned him with us. If he doesn't care enough to keep Albert, then he's not coming back. And tomorrow Tortoise Tom will come for Albert."

"How can your mother meet with him when she'll be at the fund-raiser?" I point out. "She'll be too busy."

"She's taking Albert to the fund-raiser in the sanctuary's animal trailer. Hank and other volunteers are helping transport Albert. Mom is super ed because a tortoise will be a great addition

e fund-raiser—especially one over a hundred

s old. She thinks having Albert there will boost

ations and adoptions for the other animals."

"It probably will," I agree. "But I don't want

Albert to go away."

"Neither do I." Becca takes her phone from her pocket and talks into it. "Reggie, why haven't you called me? Albert needs you! We're running out of time."

"Why the sad faces?" Dad booms as he comes into the kitchen. He peers around, probably noticing some spots of flour we missed cleaning. "Something go wrong with the cookies?"

"No, they're fine," I say.

"If it isn't about cookies, what's the problem?"

Dad's always been a great listener—maybe that's where I got the trait—so I tell him the truth. "Double bad news." I spot a chocolate stain on the counter and scrub it with a rag. "Not only is Wild Oaks losing a really cool tortoise, but tomorrow the Sparklers' face-painting booth is doomed."

"Doomed? That sounds serious." Dad wets a rag d wipes one of the counters. "Anything I can do elp?"

"Can you face paint?" I ask.

"I can't paint people, but I can paint fac
animal-face cupcakes," Dad says. "I make a d
cious snow-dog cupcake with whipped cream
sprinkles."

"Sounds yummy, but we need a face painter."

"It's all about earning money for the Humane
Society, right?" Dad points out. "Whatever you
bring in will be appreciated."

"But our booth will probably lose money since
the face paints costs so much and only Becca can
paint faces," I say.

"Tyla could paint a face in five minutes—but it
takes me fifteen." Becca groans. "Even if we raise the
price to five dollars a face, I can't paint fast enough."

"What are the hours for the fund-raiser?" Leo
asks.

"Ten to four," Becca answers.

"According to my calculations, if you paint for
six hours without taking a break you'll make one
hundred twenty dollars," Leo says.

"Almost the cost of Tyla's fancy face paints."
Becca twists her pink-streaked ponytail. "If only
we'd come up with a booth idea that everyone cou
agree on."

"Kelsey says the Sparklers all love my cookies." Dad speaks quickly, his voice rising with excitement. "Why paint faces for little profit when you can sell my cookies and donate *all* the profits? You already have three dozen of my famous ChipTastics." Dad waves his hand at our heaping cookie platters. "If we work together, we could double that amount. I've been wanting to do my part to help the fund-raiser."

"Sell cookies instead of paint faces?" Becca stares at Dad in surprise.

"Why not do both?" Dad suggests.

"And I'll help," Leo adds as he takes down a cooking apron. "I planned to go anyway. Becca can paint faces and the rest of us will sell cookies."

"Wow!" I grin. "Great idea, Dad."

"*Fantastique!*" Becca flashes a huge smile. "Thank you, Mr. Case! You may have just saved our fund-raiser."

"Anything for a good cause—and for my kids," he adds, playfully tugging on a curl of my hair. "So why are you standing around? Let's make cookies!"

Mom joins in the cookie production line. And when my sisters get home from their dance, they offer to wrap the cookies in decorative bundles. My sister Kenya does a lot of DIY (do-it-yourself) craft projects. She brings out a spool of metallic gold ribbon and ties off each bag of cookies with it. More practical than creative, but equally clever, Kiana shows us how to use the edge of the scissors to curl the ribbon into spirals.

We're all working when my brother comes in, sweaty and tired. He doesn't ask what we're doing and stomps directly into his room and closes his door.

Several hours and more than two hundred cookies later, I'm exhausted in a good way. Despite everything that went wrong today, our cookie celebration was a delicious success. After my friends leave, I sink into my bed, expecting to fall into a deep sleep.

But my brain runs like a hamster on a spinning wheel. I can't stop thinking about Albert and unsolved mysteries—like why my brother would need a lawyer. I imagine him behind bars in prison orange. I worry about Albert too. What if he dies of a broken heart? Tortoise Tom might have lots of experience with tortoises, but he's not Reggie. Albert needs his family.

Mysteries torment me too. Was it really Erik who left the ransom note and the wooden puzzle box? He never admitted it; I assumed he was guilty because the Corning Comic site was taken down.

But the wooden box with the clue to my notebook was placed in my locker *before* I talked to Erik. Why pretend he didn't know about my notebook if he'd already taken the steps to return it? And the timing of his website shutting down is weird too. He knew I'd get my notebook back and keep his secret, so why delete his website? I only asked him to take down the cartoon about Sophia.

Stop thinking and go to sleep, I tell myself. But my hamster-wheel brain circles around and around facts and questions. Finally, I snap on my light and go over to my closet. I take down my spy pack and pull out two baggies of evidence.

Evidence A: The green disk or button or game piece. I still don't know what it is, but it's the only real clue I have to what was inside my brother's large, white box. I pick the disk up and turn it over between my fingers, feeling like I've seen one of these somewhere recently. But where?

Evidence B: The ransom note with its bits of papers from magazines. There's a photo of a half-smiling, half-frowning clown face on the back of one of the "ransom" scraps and a logo from a trendy teen magazine. Erik probably has lots of magazines since he's interested in photography, but I'm surprised he'd have a fashion magazine like *InbeTWEEN*. Was I was too quick to hang a "guilty" verdict on Erik?

But if not Erik, then who?

Studying the scraps of paper, I focus on the happy-sad clown face. It has some meaning, I'm sure. But what?

One way to find out.

I toss on a robe and go into the living room and power up the computer. I put in keywords like "clown face," "smile," and "frown."

And there's the exact image on my scrap of paper.

The picture is defined as: two masks, one smiling and one frowning, generally accepted as the symbol of the two aspects of theater. The smiling mask signifies comedy, and the frowning mask signifies drama.

OMG! The drama club uses this image on their posters.

I hold the note up to my face and sniff that odd flowery-chemical scent again. I was wrong about it coming from the paper—the smell of hair spray mixed with mouthwash is coming from the glue!

The paper eyeball stares up at me, and olfactory memory (as Leo would say) takes me back a few days. I replay the sequence of events that began when I accidentally brought my notebook to school. Puzzles shift into place and I can see the big picture.

I know who's guilty.

- Chapter 22 -
Accusations

The Humane Society fund-raiser is a Case family event.

Usually we all pile into our van and go together. But since Mom is an animal control officer, she has to be there early in her animal control truck. I'm going with her since I need to be there early for the Sparkler booth.

The fund-raiser is being held at Bluff Vista Park, which has grassy acres of oaks and pines that sweep into a high bluff overlooking the Sun River. It's in an exclusive area of Sun Flower near a golf course and a fancy development of new, very large homes. When we arrive, lots of cars and official vehicles are already there, including the sheriff's patrol car and a truck and trailer from Wild Oaks Sanctuary.

Mom looks great in her uniform and beams with pride as she locks up her work truck.

"This is going to be fun," she tells me, tucking her keys in a pocket. "I can't wait to pass out brochures on responsible pet care and spay-and-neuter clinics."

"That's all you're going to do?" I ask. "Sounds boring."

"Not at all! I love giving advice and answering questions." She picks up a leather briefcase, then goes around to the back of the truck. "Also I get to run this cool machine that makes personalized pet tags."

I almost ask Mom to make a tag for Honey, but I haven't told her about my kitten. Becca's mom is the only adult who knows Honey is mine. Someday, I'll bring Honey home—when we move out of the no-pets apartment.

Mom carries a heavy box that must contain the pet tag maker, and I stack two boxes of cookies in my arms. I scan the rows of festive booths, some still in the process of being set up and others waving banners and balloons inviting visitors. Becca told me the Sparkler booth is on the third aisle at the bluff end of the park. Trees thicken around the uphill path to the bluff, which I've heard offers a gorgeous view of Sun River and would be fun to hike.

"There's my booth." Mom points to several long tables covered with a white canopy on metal poles. "If you need anything, come find me."

"Thanks, Mom." I shift my arms for a better grip on the cookie boxes.

It takes a while to find the Sparkler booth. I walk up and down aisles, admiring all the booths. While the main objective of the fund-raiser is to raise funds, the goal is also to teach people to be responsible pet owners. One booth has tables and chairs set with animal coloring books and crayons for kids. I flip through one of the books and read captions about pets that have been rescued and adopted through the Humane Society. Another booth offers free pet grooming for dogs and cats adopted during the event. There are booths just for fun too, like balloon popping. (I told the Sparklers this was a good idea, but no one would listen.)

My favorite activity is the Puppy Raceway, where the first puppy race is scheduled for noon. Puppies race around obstacles and are rewarded with treats. All the puppies in the race are up for adoption. Another activity is the Furry and Fabulous Fashion Show, where a 4-H group has made glamorous outfits for older cats and dogs who are harder to adopt. I pause at this booth to wave at a cocker mix with just three legs that barks hello.

As I weave through the aisles I see lots of familiar faces from school: Erik, Ann Marie, Tori, Mr. Thompson, and Mrs. Ross. I spot Becca's mother with Wild Oak volunteers at a large booth with animal crates. Hank and a few other men are carefully unloading Albert off a wheeled cart. I head over to see Albert but stop when I hear someone call my name.

"Kelsey!" I turn to see Leo waving from the drama club's booth. It's decorated with sets and costumes from *The Lion King*. A bulletin board announces that every hour, actors in jungle costumes will perform scenes from the play. They're raffling off gorgeous wrapped baskets on display with stuffed zoo animals and play tickets.

I spot Frankie smearing yellow face makeup on a stocky kid—I think his name is Haydon—who stars as Simba in the play. The drama teacher, Mrs. Ross, and her assistant, Perrin, struggle to fit a humongous lion headpiece on Haydon. I study

Perrin; his curly black hair is pulled back in a bandana, and he's wearing a medieval-looking puffy-sleeved shirt like a pirate. He struts around giving orders to other kids like he thinks he's the boss. I'll bet he already knew Sophia had the part when he accepted the theater tickets from her.

"Hey, Leo," I say, walking over. "What are you doing here? I thought you were going to help out with cookie sales."

"I'm waiting to talk to Frankie. But it could be a while." He gestures to Frankie, who is gluing wild-animal hair onto Simba's arms.

"Did you notice who else is here?" Frowning, I point to Perrin. "He's the reason Sophia dropped out of the play and isn't here today. I'm tempted to go tell him off."

"Don't waste your breath. Jerks like that don't care whom they hurt."

"Instead of taking the tickets from Sophia, he could have told her that she would probably get the part on her own," I say angrily. "But he's so stuck on himself, I bet he's the one who told the Corning Comic about the bribe."

"That's what Frankie thinks too."

I pause to think this over then shake my head.

"But the Corning Comic returned my notebook and was so afraid I'd expose his identity, he even took his website down."

"Um...he didn't." Leo sucks in a deep breath. "I did."

"You?" I choke out.

Leo lowers his voice, leaning closer to me. "It didn't seem right what he was doing, hurting people with cruel cartoons. I don't like bullies. So I shut him down for a few days."

"Wow" is all I can say. I know what Leo did was wrong too, but I can't help but be impressed.

"Frankie better hurry up," Leo says, abruptly changing the subject. "I promised to give him a demonstration of FRODO's olfactory directional ability."

I look at Leo's empty hands. "Where is the smelly robot?"

"He's *not* smelly," Leo says with an insulted sniff. "FRODO can identify odors better than any human. I left FRODO in Mom's car. I was going to show Frankie before I helped with the cookies, but he's too busy transforming actors into jungle animals. Isn't he great at it? He could really help the CCSC with disguises."

"I'm sure he could," I say with a twinge of guilt because I still don't want Frankie in our club.

"I'll walk with you to the Sparkler booth and talk to Frankie later," Leo says.

The Sparkler booth—really just a canopy over three tables and four chairs—is half-hidden beneath a shady oak—not an easy location for customers to find. Becca is the only one there.

"Finally, some help!" Becca rushes up to us. "Chloe just texted that she won't be here for an hour—and she has the decorations and face paints."

I frown at the two bare tables underneath a plain white canopy. No banners or colorful decorations like the other booths.

"We may not have fancy decorations to attract customers, but we have something better." I hold out the boxes in my arms. "ChipTastic cookies!"

"Yummm. They smell amazing," Becca says with a happy sniff.

"I'll be your first customer." Leo pulls out a wallet from his pocket. "How much are the cookies?"

"Five tickets a bag," Becca says. "But before any cookies are sold, we need to set up the booth."

She shows me where I can display the cookies. I arrange them on a rectangular table while Leo hangs the Sparkler banner—the only decoration we have until Chloe shows up—over the top of the booth. Becca sets out chairs and a small table for face painting. I borrow some paper and a pen from another booth to post the price of the cookies. While I'm working, I sneak peeks at my friends, wondering if I should tell them who stole my notebook now or wait till later.

It's going to be a shock—and one of them isn't going to like it. Maybe I should wait till after the fund-raiser or tomorrow...or never.

This isn't a secret I can write down in my notebook and keep to myself. I've solved a mystery, and they both need to know. Then we need to confront the thief.

So when we finish arranging the booth and Leo starts to leave to buy tickets, I put my hand on his arm. "Wait," I say. "Could you sit down? You too, Becca. I need to tell you something important."

"What?" they both ask.

"I know who stole my notebook." They stare at me with dropping jaws and widening eyes. I rush on before I lose my nerve. "My first suspect was Tyla until I figured out it couldn't be her. Next I suspected Erik, since he's the Corning Comic and posted that secret about Sophia. But I wondered why he'd shut down his own website if he had my secrets—unless he never had them" I give Leo a meaningful look. "I realized Sophia's secret going viral had nothing to do with my notebook."

"How else did Erik find out about Sophia?" A crease deepens between Becca's brows.

"Mrs. Ross's assistant, Perrin, probably told him. I think Perrin took that information to the Corning Comic, hoping to get something in return."

"So who did steal your notebook?" Becca says.

This is the hard part. It was easy to suspect Erik since he isn't a close friend and he had M-O-M: motive, opportunity, and means. But the guilty person is someone close to one of my CCSC friends. I clench my hands together. "The ransomer is—"

"Ransomer is not a real word," Leo interrupts.

"It is for us," Becca argues. "Shush! Let her finish."

"I studied my clues and realized a connection between a photo on my ransom note and a suspect. Also there was an odd smell from the ransom note, and I knew who was guilty." I look directly at Leo and drop the bomb from my lips. "Frankie."

"Absolutely not." Leo glares. "Frankie had no

reason to steal your notebook."

"He's the only one who could have," I say sadly.

"You've never liked him and are being totally unfair!" Leo's face reddens with outrage. "You have no proof."

"The glue on the ransom note has a weird smell—like hair spray and mouthwash. The same smell that came from the glue on Frankie's desk. It's probably some special glue for actors. And one of the magazine photos used for the ransom note had a theater mask symbol on the back—the same symbol I saw backstage."

"Frankie did not steal your notebook!" Leo glares at me like I'm his worse enemy. "It could have been anyone in the drama club."

"He did it out of revenge," I insist. "I didn't vote for him to join our club so he stole my notebook."

"He did *not!*" Leo shouts so loudly that a family passing us stops to stare.

Becca lowers her voice. "Kelsey could be right."

"Not you too! I'm not going to listen to your lies!" Leo throws up his hands, then storms past the cookie table and out of the booth.

I jump up to go after him but Becca pulls me back into the chair. "He needs time to cool off."

"Leo hates me," I say with an aching heart.

"No, he doesn't, but he won't believe you without proof."

"I don't know how to prove it, but I'm sure Frankie is guilty. He had opportunity—hanging out with Leo let him know what we were doing. Means—he could easily find out my locker combination. And revenge for keeping him out of the club is a strong motive."

"All guesses—not proof," Becca says, and she's right.

But how do I find proof? I puzzle over that. The glue smell and mask photo are good clues but not enough to convince Leo. It would be more convincing if I could find a copy of *InbeTWEEN* magazine in Frankie's possession—especially if there are cutout words and pictures. But where would he keep it? His home? Locker? Backstage office?

Before I can come up with a plan, customers lured by the sweet scent of ChipTastics arrive. While Becca takes tickets, I hand out the cookie bags. Some customers remember Dad from when he worked at Café Belmond. A petite young woman with angel designs on her jacket says she used to stop by Café Belmond for Dad's croissants. "Your father is a culinary genius!" she raves, then buys *ten* bags of cookies.

We're super busy until Chloe shows up with the decorations and face paints.

Chloe decorates the booth, then takes over the ticket-collecting so Becca can paint faces. While I hand out cookies, I keep looking through the sea of faces, hoping to see Leo.

Finally, when sales slow down (probably because the animal fashion show has started), I push away from the table and tell Becca I'm going to look for Leo.

"He's probably at the drama club booth," she says.

I nod grimly. "With Frankie."

But when I get there, I only find Mrs. Ross and some actors in jungle animal costumes. No Frankie or Leo.

"Excuse me, Mrs. Ross." I tap her shoulder.

The teacher's long snake-like braid whips around as she turns toward me. "I'm kind of busy here, Kelsey."

"I'm looking for Frankie and Leo," I say quickly.

"They were here about an hour ago. They talked for a while, then suddenly Frankie took off running. He left so fast that he dropped his cap." She gestures to a table where I see a familiar green cap. "Leo ran after him, and that's the last I saw of them."

Alarm shivers through me. "You don't know where they are?"

She shakes her head. "I've tried calling Frankie's cell, but he doesn't answer. The actors are performing in twenty minutes, and I need Frankie's help with the costumes."

"I'll go look for them," I say.

"Thanks, dear. When you see Frankie, tell him to hurry back. It's almost time for our first performance. Oh, and give him this." She hands me the green cap.

Turning the cap over in my hands, I get a bad feeling. I've never seen Frankie without this hat. Holding it tight, I start searching for the boys.

I start at the entrance and go through aisles, peering in every booth. When I pass the Wild Oaks Sanctuary booth, I see a group of parents with their kids admiring and snapping photos of Albert. The tortoise lifts his head, as if trying to be friendly, but his eyes are sad. I want to go over and comfort him, but I have to find the boys.

Weaving through the crowded aisles, I swivel my head back and forth, searching.

No sign of Frankie or Leo anywhere.

Could they be in the boys' restroom? But going there could be awkward. Still, it's the only place I haven't checked. I wait outside, watching two guys go in and a father with a small son exit. When the two guys come out moments later, I'm sure no one is inside—unless Frankie and Leo went in there to talk privately.

I bite my lip and wonder, *One little peek can't hurt...Right?*

I glance around to make sure no one is watching, then cautiously open the door. "Uh...Frankie? Leo? Are you here?"

A deep adult voice calls back, "No!"

I slam the door fast and run away.

With my hands on my hips, I look around all the booths, growing worried. Where are those boys? I remember Leo saying he wanted to show Frankie his smelling robot. Of course. With renewed hope, I head for the parking lot. It's so crowded that some cars are parked on the dirt. I go up and down the rows of vehicles, looking into every vehicle.

Still no Leo or Frankie.

Could they have returned to the drama club booth? I start back but stop when I hear a shout. I turn and there's Leo, running toward me.

"*Leo!*" I'm so happy to see him that I throw my arms around him—until I realize that I'm hugging a *boy*. I jump back. My face burns hot with embarrassment.

Leo's face is red too, but probably because he's been running.

"Have you seen Frankie?" he asks me in a rush.

"I was going to ask you the same thing."

Leo's blond hair is mussed, sweat drips from his forehead, and there's dirt on his black slacks. "I've lost Frankie."

"What happened?" I ask.

"He wanted to know why I was angry at you and Becca, so I told him the truth." Leo's shoulders slump. "I expected him to get angry and say you were wrong—but he didn't. Instead he looked scared and then ran from me...like a guilty person. I chased after him through the aisles, but when he headed up for the bluff path, I lost him. I must have hiked the trails for an hour, calling his name and looking everywhere. But there are too many trails, and I couldn't see much through the dense trees.

Finally, I turned around and came here."

"Why the parking lot?" I ask, glancing around.

"Mom's car is here." He walks to a cream-colored Sorento and pulls a key from his pocket.

"You can't drive," I say.

"Actually I can, but I'm beneath the age limit and a car can't go where I'm going." He pops open the car trunk. "Frankie is somewhere in those trees, and FRODO will lead me to him."

- Chapter 23 -
Follow That Smell!

"Will this help?" I show Leo the green cap Mrs. Ross gave me.

"Frankie's hat! Thanks. His scent will be strong on this." Leo tucks it and FRODO under his arm and hurries toward the hill.

"Wait!" I grab him by the arm.

He shakes me off. "I have to find Frankie."

"Not alone. I'm going with you."

"But you don't even like him."

"I don't dislike him—I just don't trust him. Besides, he's your friend and I want to help you find him." I glance back at the colorful tents and crowds. "We should let someone know where we're going in case we get lost."

"It's impossible to get lost with FRODO to guide us."

The parking lot rises below the park and a path leads high into hills, mostly to walking trails leading to a cliff overlooking the river.

"What will you do with Frankie's cap?" I hurry to keep in step with Leo as he heads up the hill where weeds and trees thicken into eerie shadows.

"FRODO will follow the scent, starting from where I lost Frankie's trail."

"Why not wait for Frankie to return on his own?"

"He should have come back by now. Frankie knew the drama group was going to perform soon. He wouldn't have abandoned them."

"You never know how someone will react when they're upset," I point out. "I'm sorry I was right about him."

"Why would he steal your notebook?" Leo pauses to catch his breath. "It's illogical. He told me he likes you."

"Even though I wouldn't vote him into our club?"

"He doesn't know. I hoped you'd change your mind so I only told him the requirements for new members."

"Oh." Now I really feel guilty. "I guess we'll find out his motive when we find him."

"*If* we find him." Leo worries as we climb a trail into shadowed trees. "I have a bad feeling."

To hear Leo say this shoots a jolt of fear through me. Leo operates on facts, not emotions. And I get a bad feeling too.

We follow the main path, which is well traveled and smooth. Just as I spot the fork in the path he told me about, I hear the sound of footsteps pounding behind us. Leo hears it too, because he stops, hope rising on his face.

"Frankie?" he calls as he whirls around.

Wrong, I think, seeing Becca approach. She's out of breath, her face reddened from running.

"I saw you running up here and hurried to catch up. What's going on?" Becca bends over slightly, resting with her arms balanced on her knees. "I wasn't sure I could catch up with you."

"Frankie is missing."

"I'll help you look for him," Becca says.

"Great," Leo says. Then he lifts his hand in the CCSC signal.

Becca and I make the hand signal too, and then we bump fists. I smile at my club mates. Solving mysteries is better with friends.

Leo leads the way, slowing only when we reach a fork in the path. Three trails branch out— right, left, and straight ahead for the cliffs. But the narrow cliff trail looks like it was made for animals, not humans, and disappears into rising boulders. Unfortunately, this is the trail Leo takes. We follow, ducking under prickly branches and climbing rough boulders, until we reach a plateau of rock.

"This is where I lost him," Leo says.

He sets FRODO down, clicks buttons on the remote, then presses the green cap to FRODO's sensors (which look like eyeballs).

A colored button flashes green and an arrow points straight ahead—where there's no path. When I look closer, I see trampled grass and a broken branch.

"Follow FRODO," Leo says.

And we do.

We wind through trees, turning right and left, and pushing away thick bushes. We're so high now that I can hear the rush from the river far below the cliffs. Kids are warned to stay away from Sun River and told that if the undercurrents don't drag you down, the chilly water will freeze you to death.

"He has to be up ahead," Leo says, pointing to dense trees. "Unless he doubled back, he must be beyond those trees."

The ground dips and drops into rocky crevices, so we have to crawl part of the way. My hands are scraped when we get through the rocky path and stand beneath the towering trees.

"So where is he?" Becca frowns.

"Not here." I shrug, looking around.

"I don't understand." Leo presses a button on his remote. "FRODO's indicators say that Frankie is *here*. The arrow points ahead to the cliff. We're on the cliff, but he's nowhere in sight. There's no way else for Frankie to go."

"But there is," I say as fear slices through me.

And I point to the cliff.

- Chapter 24 -
Cliffhanger

A scraggy tree hangs at an odd angle over the edge of empty air. Soft dirt shimmers with mossy-green dew and crumbly rocks. One patch of dirt is scuffed with skid marks disappearing over the cliff—like something or someone has fallen.

"*OMG!*" I cry.

Becca grabs for my hand, horror reflecting in her dark eyes.

"Frankie." Leo's gasp tumbles like a heavy rock from his gaping mouth.

We're frozen in what seems like forever, staring at empty sky beyond the cliff. In my mind, I see it happening: Frankie running, too upset to watch where he's going until he's sliding on the cliff's edge, the mossy grass slippery. His arms flail as the ground crumbles beneath him and he falls...

"It's too horrible!" Becca sobs and throws her arms around me. "No one was here to help...He didn't have a chance."

"Poor Frankie." My heart aches as I look over at Leo who just stands there, staring at the cliff.

"We should do something," Becca says.

I nod, tears stinging my face.

Leo is made of stone, saying nothing. Neither of us makes a move to look over the edge. Like when I went to my grandfather's funeral and couldn't bear to look inside his coffin.

Did Frankie land on the rocks, or is the river his coffin?

I walk over to Leo, touching his arm. "We...we should go for help."

"Help..."

I'm staring at Leo's face but his lips haven't moved.

"Help..." I hear the faint cry again.

Leo must have heard it too, because he's rushing to the cliff's edge and kneeling over to look down.

"*Frankie!*" he screams.

Snapping out of my shock, I run over beside

him, careful not to get too close to the edge as I peer over.

Then I see him, a blue stripe of hair on dark black and a face so pale he could be a ghost—except that he's alive! Frankie clings to a root with both hands, one foot perched on a tiny rock jutting from the cliff and the other dangling over a steep drop down to a ribbon of river. If he falls, he's dead.

"I'll pull you up," Leo shouts down.

"I'll help." Becca leans over, twisting the end of her black ponytail.

"We all will," I add. "Hang on, Frankie!"

"What do you think I've been doing?" Frankie calls up in a shaky voice.

Leo bends over, stretching as far as he can. But there's about a two-foot gap between Leo's reaching fingers and Frankie's grasping hands.

When Leo turns to me, his face is ashen with terror. "We need help!"

"I left my phone at the booth," Becca says with a helpless gesture.

"Leo, what about your phone?" I ask.

He takes it from his pocket, then hangs his head in shame. "No power...So much happened last night that I forgot to charge it."

I don't know if I'm more shocked that Frankie is dangling over the cliff or that organized Leo forgot to charge his phone.

But my brain clicks into calm clarity, and I say, "I'll run back to the fund-raiser and get help."

Becca shakes her head. "No, you stay here with Frankie. I'll run to my mom's booth and get Hank and the other volunteers to help."

"Tell them to bring rope," Leo adds.

"Leo," Frankie calls up feebly. "Go...get... Mom."

"I won't leave you," Leo insists.

"You...you're the only one who...who knows Mom." Frankie sucks in a weary breath, his knuckles white as he clutches the tree. "Get Mom... please."

Leo's face is grim as he nods. Then he and Becca are running, disappearing into trees. And it's just Frankie and me.

I'm sweating fear but trying to stay calm as I kneel down on the dirt. I hang my head over the ledge.

"Frankie, are you okay?"

"Never better." His laugh is more like a gasp.

"Hold on tight."

"Yeah." He's clinging awkwardly to the branch,

his face streaked with dirt. "I am...but...getting tired."

"You're doing great. Help will be here soon," I say, hoping my words are true. I worry he's weakening. "Don't give up."

"I never...never give up," he says, then adds in a ragged voice. "I'm sorry."

"Sorry for falling off a cliff?"

"That too...but not what I meant." His grip on the root slips and he grabs at it, dirt tumbling like dark snow around him.

"Save your energy," I call out, fear clutching my heart.

"But...but in case"—a groan—"if I can't hold on long enough...I want you to know I never meant to hurt anyone."

"Is this some kind of confession? Well, forget it," I say furiously because he's scaring me. "Save the confession until later. Your safety is way more important than a stupid notebook."

"Leo said you know I took it," Frankie chokes out.

"That doesn't matter now."

"But it does—to me. I want you to know why."

"I don't care why you did it. Just hold on and save your energy."

"Talking helps keep...keep me from freaking out."

"Okay, then talk. Do *not* freak out. Do *not* fall!"

"Not on my to-do list." He gulps. "Besides, things I mean to do don't always work out. I only took the notebook to impress you."

"There are better ways to impress me," I say with a groan. "Stealing isn't on the list."

"It was supposed to be fun. Leo said members in your club had to be"—he sucks in a raspy breath— "good at puzzles, solving mysteries, and being trustworthy."

"You stole my notebook so I'd trust you?" I ask in confusion.

His grip on the branch is so fragile that I clench my hands together as if I can hold on for him. "It was a spy game," he finally says so softly that I strain my ears to hear. "I took the notebook so you could follow clues to finding it—like the games Leo told me you did in your club."

"Leo told you about our spy games!" I exclaim.

"Not much...just that you...you tested him and Becca." He pauses to catch his breath, then talks fast as if he's running out of time. "I thought if I did the same for you, you'd want me in your club. After Tyla shouted that you had secrets in your notebook, I followed you to your locker, spying to learn your locker combination. I took your notebook, then pieced together a ransom note from magazines."

"*InbeTWEEN* magazine was one of them," I say.

"Yeah." His voice seems weaker.

"I figured out you were guilty because of the glue." I need to keep talking, encouraging him to hang on. "You used a stinky glue."

"Spirit glue. Actors use it for putting beards and hair on faces. The school buys a stinky brand because it's cheaper." He starts to laugh, but it turns into a cough when dirt falls into his mouth. When he can talk again, he continues. "I was so proud of my ransom note—my first ever."

"My first too," I admit. "But why lead me to a closed donut shop and then not return my notebook?"

"It wasn't about the notebook; it was about the dog. I saw that dog in the park on the way to school...a lost pet." He coughs. "So I left school a little early—I can do that since drama is my last class—and caught the dog. I left him for you to find, so you could get the reward for your club."

"Wow" is all I can say.

"You were supposed to find the notebook by following the puzzle-box clue."

"I couldn't figure it out."

"Didn't you ask Leo for help?" He moves his hands slightly and dirt tumbles down, down, down to the distant river below. I squeeze my eyes shut, terrified. When I open my eyes, I focus on Frankie's face as he continues talking. "I thought Leo and Becca would help you solve the puzzle."

"I didn't show it to them right away," I admit.

He doesn't say anything, his glance shifting down toward the river below.

"Look up at me! Hold on! Don't you want to know why I didn't show the box to Leo and Becca?" I speak fast and loud, desperate to keep him gazing up at me.

"Yeah," he says feebly. "Tell me."

"Leo was busy with you, and Becca had the Sparklers. So I tried to prove I didn't need their help. But it turns out I did." I think back. "I thought Erik Taylor stole my notebook because of the Corning Comic's cartoon about Sophia. But you already know Erik is the Corning Comic since you read the notebook."

"No." He starts to shake his head, but that makes his fingers slip so he goes still. "I know now...but didn't." His words come out in ragged gasps. "I didn't read...your notebook."

"But you must have! All those secrets—how could you resist?"

"I glanced...but I didn't read...well...until I saw Leo's name...couldn't believe he's only eleven."

"Almost twelve," I point out.

"In three weeks," Frankie whispers. "He doesn't want a party."

"He's embarrassed about his age." I frown. "Does he know you know?"

"No...Age doesn't matter...He's the best friend I ever had." He sucks in a ragged breath, then continues. "He said you'd let me join the club if I could solve mysteries, help animals, and earn your trust. The puzzle box was a mystery, and I found the lost dog. I didn't read your secrets—except Leo's—so I'm trustworthy." He breathes in and out slowly. "And I left a new secret...never even told Leo. Can I...I be in your club?"

I really feel low, like a slimy bug that deserves to be squished. So what if he stole my notebook? He didn't do it out of meanness, but to prove himself to the CCSC. And I was too suspicious and unforgiving to give him a chance.

Frankie makes a choking sound. There's a horrible sound of dirt falling.

"Hold on!" I lean over the edge, desperately looking for a way to reach him. But he's too far down...and slipping. His foot gives way. He dangles in midair, held up only by a sagging tree root that showers a dirt waterfall.

"Can't...hold on...much longer..." Frankie gasps.

I look around desperately. I have to help him! But what can I do? I can't risk leaning over any further because the rocky dirt I'm kneeling on isn't very firm. I can't reach him.

Ohmygod! What if he falls and all I can do is watch?

My heart pounds as if it's trying to escape from my chest. I stare down at Frankie, no longer seeing a boy who can't be trusted...but a friend I may lose.

"I'm sorry," I tell him. "Just hang on, and when you're safe, we'll take a vote on letting you into the CCSC. You have my vote. I promise."

"Really?" Hope shines from his mud-streaked face.

"Yeah." I nod. "Your ransom note was cool. The

puzzle box really clever. And catching a fast dog like Bobbsey proves you're good at helping animals. You'll make a great addition to the CCSC."

He smiles feebly. "What...what does CCSC stand for?"

"Leo didn't tell you?"

"No...a...club secret." His voice is so weak I can barely hear him.

"It's the Curious Cat—"

I don't get any further because there's a shout from behind me.

When I turn, I see Leo, Becca, her mother, Hank, and a stocky man wearing a red bolo tie.

Help is here!

Chapter 25

Tortoise Tom

A heavy rope dangles from Hank's callused hands, and he offers the end of it to the man wearing a bolo tie. Bolo Tie Man ties the rope on a tree trunk, his thick fingers twisting the rope into a complicated knot.

"Hold on, son!" Hank calls out as he carries the loose end of the rope to the cliff.

I stand on wobbly legs, reluctant to lift my gaze from Frankie as if I'm holding him up by sheer will. But I move away from the cliff to give the strong men plenty of room for the rescue. I squeeze between Becca and her mother.

Mrs. Morales shouts down to Frankie, "We'll get you out."

"You're going to be okay," Becca adds.

Frankie opens his mouth to reply, but I hear nothing except the terrified pounding of my own heart.

Hank tosses the rope down to Frankie. "Grab hold of it," he says gently.

"I'm...I'm afraid to let go," Frankie sobs.

"You can do it," Becca encourages.

"Take the rope!" I cry.

"I don't wanna fall..." His voice cracks. "Where's my mom?"

"She's coming," Becca answers. "Leo is bringing her. But you need to focus on getting up here. Take the rope, Frankie."

"I'll loop it so you can let it drop over your head," Hank calls out. "Once it's on your waist it'll tighten, and you can grab hold of the rope while I pull you up."

Frankie sobs, but he doesn't argue.

Becca, her mother, and I stand back. We cling to each other, watching the two men ease the rope down to Frankie. When I hear a cry and the sound of falling dirt, I grit my teeth hard so I don't cry out.

There's a scraping sound. Shouts. The rope is

lifted. And when I see a blue curl over Frankie's black hair, I whoop for joy. He's safe!

A woman screams Frankie's name, and Leo appears with a woman who looks just like Frankie—same raven black hair and dark eyes. She rushes forward to Frankie, sobbing and laughing as she throws her arms around her son.

"Mom!" he cries, hugging her.

It gets crazy after that with more adults coming forward to help, but fortunately the danger is over. We're a strange parade of adults and kids as we wind back down the woodsy path to the festive booths. The Humane Society fund-raiser continues, with only a small group aware of how close this fun event came to becoming a tragedy.

Leo refuses to leave Frankie's side, and they go with the flow of concerned adults. I turn to Becca. "I guess we should get back to the Sparkler booth."

"Not yet," she says. "We need to go to my mom's booth."

"Why?"

She frowns. "He's leaving."

From her sad expression, I immediately know who she's talking about.

Bolo-Tie Man is Tortoise Tom—and he's come to

take Albert away. All my happiness at Frankie's rescue fades away.

"You must be the kids who've been helping this fine tortoise," Tortoise Toms greets us, smiling. "What an amazing creature! I haven't seen an Aldabra that old and in such great shape for years. You've done a wonderful job caring for him."

"Not us," I say softly. "His owner, Reggie, took great care of him."

"But didn't keep him," Becca's mother puts in, her expression critical. "Albert will be happy with Thomas."

"That he will," Thomas booms, the strings on his red bolo tie wiggling. "No worries about the tortoise. He'll get the best care possible. And as a bonus, he'll have the company of some lovely female Aldabra tortoises."

But he won't be with his best friend, I think sadly.

"You kids go say your good-byes," Thomas tells us. "I'm in no hurry to leave. I'm going to check out the food booths. I heard there's some award-winning chili that sounds delicious."

After he leaves, Becca and I walk over to the makeshift tortoise pen. Albert is beside a shallow tub of water. His head is tucked in like he's sleeping. I call his name and he doesn't move. Becca tries too, but still no response. So we call him together, and his wrinkly neck lifts toward us.

"Let's get closer to him," Becca says, stepping over the gate.

We kneel next to Albert, stroking his neck and speaking to him softly. We say encouraging things, like how cool his new home will be and how popular he'll be with his new girlfriends. His black eyes study us, but they're like gray clouds darkening as the skies prepare to storm.

"So everything turned out great," I tell Becca in a forced upbeat tone. "Frankie was rescued. Dad's cookies are a hit. And the mystery of my missing notebook is solved—Frankie explained why he took it."

While we sit on each side of Albert, I tell Becca everything Frankie said. When I'm finished, her eyes practically pop out. "He did it to impress us?" She flips her ponytail over her shoulder. "Seriously, that's the craziest thing I've ever heard."

"It worked though, because I am impressed. Not only did he come up with creative clues, but he was so stealth that I never suspected him."

"But aren't you mad he stole your notebook? Now he knows your secrets—and one of mine."

"No, he doesn't." I say. "He didn't read our secrets so he doesn't know about your mo—"

"My mother," she finishes, biting her lip.

"Yeah. Do you want to know her secret?" I ask as I gently stroke Albert.

"I've suspected something fishy was up with her. She's been acting weird lately, wearing perfume and fussing with her hair. She's dating someone, isn't she?"

I nod. "Are you okay with that?"

"As long as it's not another cowboy," she says with a wry smile.

"It's not." It feels weird to talk about my secrets. I'm so used to hiding them, but I want to be honest with Becca. So I tell her about seeing her mother kissing the sheriff, and she doesn't freak out.

"I guess that's not too bad," she says, looking relieved. "I like the sheriff."

We're quiet for a few minutes, and my thoughts drift back to Frankie.

"There's something else I have to tell you," I say to Becca.

"Are *you* dating someone?" she teases.

"Me? No way." I laugh. "But I told Frankie I'd vote for him to join the CCSC."

"I thought you didn't want any new members."

"True," I admit. "The three of us are the perfect team, and I love our club the way it is. But Leo really wants Frankie to join."

"Do you want me to vote him in?" Becca reaches into a food bin, picking up a carrot that she offers to Albert. He sniffs, then turns his head away.

I frown, not sure what to say. I don't want our club to change, but Frankie is clever, resourceful, and great with disguises. I sigh. "Vote for him," I say.

Becca gets a thoughtful look on her face. "I have an idea about how to keep things the same and yet change too."

"What?"

"We vote Frankie in as an associate member."

"Associate?" I wrinkle my brow. "What does that mean?"

"Frankie joins our club, but you, me, and Leo are still the main members. The three of us will meet after school like we do now, but when we have a mystery to solve or go out looking for lost pets, our associate member can join us."

I grin. "We'll change *and* stay the same. I love it!"

A short while later, Mrs. Morales, Hank, and Tortoise Tom return.

"Get your good-byes said?" Tom asks, wiping chili from his shirt and licking it off his finger.

Becca and I nod, stepping away from Albert.

It seems like so much is changing too fast. Albert is going away and I may never see him again. Leo doesn't sit alone at lunch anymore, and his new friend will join our club. The CCSC is changing, but with baby steps.

Change takes times to get used to, like sitting with the Sparklers and being temporarily part of their group. Friendships change too, rising and falling, then coming back together stronger than ever.

Next week I'll go back to sitting with Tori and Ann Marie at lunch. But my afternoons will be all about the CCSC with Becca, Leo, and sometimes Frankie.

I glance up at Becca as she hugs Albert, the Carapace Chic scrunchie in her hair shimmery in silvery gray and tan like the Aldabra's shell.

I come beside Becca and wrap my arms around Albert too.

As I get ready for bed that night, I'm feeling pretty good. Frankie is safe, the Sparkler booth made more money than expected, Albert has a good home with Tortoise Tom, and the CCSC solved another mystery.

I'm pulling back my comforter when I hear a tap on my door. Mom comes in and hands me the phone. "It's Becca," she says and closes the door behind her.

"Sorry for calling so late but this can't wait," Becca says in an excited rush.

"What?" I sit on the edge of my bed.

"Frankie found him!" She practically screams so that I have to pull the phone away from my ear.

"Huh?" I'm not sure I heard right. "Frankie found who? Start at the beginning."

Becca sucks in a deep breath. "Remember how Frankie found Reggie's agent and I left a message with her for Reggie?"

"Right. But Reggie never called back."

"Well, Frankie wanted to prove he could solve a mystery, so he contacted a friend of his mother's — she used to work at a Hollywood talent agency. The friend tracked Reggie down to a remote desert location, and Reggie just called me!"

"Yay!" I do a little happy dance.

"I nearly fell over when I heard Reggie's voice on the phone," Becca goes on excitedly.

"He explained everything and apologized for not contacting us sooner."

"Why didn't he?" I think of Albert's sad dark eyes and how much he missed Reggie.

"He's been working in the desert without a cell signal. He hadn't gotten the message from his agent. Frankie's friend had to call several people just to get a message to him. When Reggie found out Tortoise Tom had Albert, he called him right away and they worked out a deal."

"What kind of a deal?"

"Reggie's career is going strong so he plans to move to LA, but he can't keep Albert until he's settled. So Albert will stay with Tortoise Tom for a while and Reggie will pay expenses. Whenever Reggie gets time off, he'll drive up to visit. Reggie cried when he told me Albert is part of his family. He said once he gets him back, he'll never let him go again. Then he told me about the film he's making and said I could tell you and Leo about it," Becca adds with a squeal. She says it's an Indiana Jones–type adventure but on the moon.

The movie won't be out for a year, so Reggie has sworn us to secrecy.

That night I take my notebook of secrets out of the hidden drawer. I was reluctant to write it in again, but where else can I put down important secrets?

I flip to the last page and lift my pen, ready to write, when I see unfamiliar printing. Frankie's writing, I know immediately, and I remember him saying he gave me a secret of his own.

> Secret 36. When I was a toddler, I was in diaper commercials and famous as "Rank Frank." I did air freshener, mouthwash, and soap commercials, and even some about farting. Funny when you're a little kid, but embarrassing when you get older. By age eight, I wasn't cute anymore. No one would hire a kid known for being stinky. So we left LA and moved to Sun Flower. I liked being a normal kid and kept "Rank Frank" a secret. No one knows I was once famous—except you.

Frankie is Rank Frank! I remember those commercials because they made me giggle. But I never

would have guessed Frankie was that little stink-
bomb kid.

His secret is safe with me, I think as I slip the
notebook into the hidden drawer.

Then I climb into bed with a smile full of secrets.

- Chapter 26 -
Unmasked

The next morning Dad announces "Special Order Day," which means we can all request our favorite breakfast and he'll make individual orders like our home is a fancy restaurant. I can't decide between frosted-flakes French toast or a fruit blast smoothie, so Dad makes me both.

By the time everyone has their special orders, it's practically lunch.

Kyle glances at the clock and jumps up from the table. "Got to go!"

He doesn't say where, but Mom and Dad nod like they understand and my brother dashes out of the room. I make an excuse to get up from the table and follow him to his bedroom, spying around a corner until he steps out into the hall.

And guess what's tucked under his arm?

A large white box.

I have a good idea where he's going, and I will *not* lose him this time.

As I hop on my bike, Kyle is already pedaling around the corner. He obeys all traffic rules as usual so it doesn't take long to catch up with him. With spinning wheels and pumping legs, I follow, staying back about a block so he won't spot me.

He stops for a red light—and even for a green light that is close to turning yellow. I duck behind a parked truck, peeking out until the light changes to green again. Then I look around for Kyle—but he's gone.

I want to scream in frustration until I realize it doesn't matter because I know he's going to the mini mall. If I hurry, maybe I can catch up with him.

But when I get to the mall, I don't see my brother or his bike anywhere.

I'm sure he went into a building—and I have a good idea which one.

Swallowing courage, I lock up my bike and stride over to the law office. The same witchy receptionist guards her legal lair. I walk right inside and storm past her to the hallway.

"Wait! Stop!" she calls but I ignore her.

I look up and down the hall, glancing inside two open doors and seeing only empty rooms. But the door at the end of the hall is closed. There's nowhere else for Kyle to go. He has to be in there.

Still, this is a lawyer's office—serious stuff happens behind these doors. How can I just burst in without an appointment? I hesitate for only a split-second before I hear the receptionist shouting. It's now or never.

So I reach out, twist the handle, and push the door open...

A woman wearing a pale-pink suit is bending over a briefcase on a table. Across from her is a tall teenage boy with light-brown hair. Is this the boy Talla was talking about? He looks *nothing* like Kyle.

So where's my brother?

Before the pink-suited lawyer can interrogate me, I whirl around. I run out of the law office so fast that humiliation can't catch up with me.

Breathing hard, I go back to my bike, ready to quit my search and go home.

But movement in front of Prehistoric Pizza catches my eye. I smile at the familiar dino face. Maybe Talla saw my brother. I can't get any more embarrassed than I already am.

"Talla," I call out, coming over to the green-scaled dinosaur. "It's me again."

The dino girl waves her promotional billboard like a hello.

"Have you seen my brother?" I ask, my breath starting to slow to normal.

She shakes her dino head, green scales shimmery in the sunlight.

"But he just came by here," I say, frustrated. "I know he did. You must have seen him ride by on his bike."

She turns away, shaking her costumed head and gesturing for me to leave.

My shoulders slump and I turn around.

A thought hits me, and I turn back. I study the tiny, round scales on the dinosaur costume. Green, shiny scales exactly like the tiny, green disk I found in Kyle's white box—a box big enough for a dino costume. There's something different about Talla. She's taller with broad shoulders, not talkative, and instead of hazel eyes, hers are brown—like my eyes.

"*Kyle!*" I say accusingly, pointing.

Dino backs away, moving toward the Prehistoric

Pizza entrance. But a costumed dinosaur can't move as fast as a determined sister.

"It is you, Kyle!" I say as I come around to block him.

"Quiet!" My brother shushes me with his finger to his dino lips. "Don't shout my name. All my coworkers call me K. C. It's bad enough having to wear this crazy costume, but it would be brutal if the guys at school found out."

"But why hide a job? You should be proud of it," I say. "Do Mom and Dad know?"

"Yeah," he admits. "But they haven't seen me in the costume. It's so embarrassing."

I know all about being embarrassed, I think with a shudder and a glance toward the lawyer's office.

"So why work here if you don't like it?" I reach out to smooth my finger over Kyle's green-scaled arm.

"I'm saving money for college and was lucky to get a job I could do on weekends and after school. I had hoped to deliver pizzas but I don't have a car," Kyle adds with a wince.

"I saw you carrying a white box out to your bike a few days ago." I hesitate, not wanting to admit I also snooped in his room. "Was your costume inside?"

"Yes." He lifts his floppy tail. "I keep it at work unless it needs to be cleaned. I had a pizza-sauce accident a few days ago and had to take it to the dry cleaners—which wasn't easy on a bike."

I glance around the parking lot and shops. "So where is your bike?"

"My boss lets me keep it in a back storage room." He gestures toward the alley beside Prehistoric Pizza, and then he itches his head. "Sometimes I clean bathrooms and mop floors, but lately it's all about this stuffy costume."

"I think it's adorable." I laugh. "I'll call you Dino Kyle."

"No! Kelsey, you can't do that to me. Don't tell anyone you saw me here." He clasps his clawed hands as if begging. "Please."

"I won't," I promise, crisscrossing my chest.

As I ride off a few minutes later, I'm grinning.

Another secret for my notebook.

When I get back home, I can smell a celebration even before I step into my house. Dad must be baking his special Happy Everything cake—with so many amazing flavors that I don't know what ingredients he uses but it's delicious.

My sisters pounce on me when I step into the living room, tugging me toward the kitchen. They usually scoff at wearing look-a-like clothes but are both in identical purple, silky pajamas and purple ballet-styled slippers. Kenya's black hair is twisted in a braid though, while Kiana's ponytail is tied at the top of her hair so it looks like an erupting black volcano.

"What's going on?" I look back and forth between their excited faces.

"*Dad has a job!*" they both scream.

I scream too and hug them, and we all dance right there in the living room. We haven't danced like this since we were little kids, and it's great. Mom joins in a few moments later, twirling me beneath her arm. My family has their faults, but when things get rough or wonderful, we support each other, and I love them.

After I catch my breath, I race into the kitchen where Dad is wearing an apron and whipping a concoction in a silver bowl.

"Congratulations!" I say, swaying back and forth like I'm still dancing.

"I'm pretty excited." He grins. "And it's all your fault."

"Me?" I touch my chest. "What did I do?"

"You used my recipe to make a few hundred cookies—which sold out yesterday at the fundraiser."

I nod, already knowing this. Face painting lost money but the cookies, which Dad donated, made a huge profit. Becca told me that Tyla didn't even apologize for not helping, but she convinced Sophia to come back to the Sparklers and stay in the play. The play starts next week, and I'm looking forward to seeing Sophia perform. I don't have to be a Sparkler to be her friend.

"While I was watching the puppy races yesterday," Dad continues, "a woman came over to compliment me on my cookies. We got to talking, and when she found out I was looking for a job, she offered me one as a personal chef to her employer. And I accepted."

"Wow!" I jump up excitedly. "Best news ever!"

"Even better." Dad sets down the mixing bowl and looks into my face. "The family I'll be working for owns a chain of resort hotels and lives on a large estate north of town in the hills."

"That's near Becca's home!" I exclaim.

"Yes, I think it is." Dad pokes his finger in the frothy concoction and licks his finger. "Just right. Anyway, the house is a modern castle with a huge kitchen just waiting for me. And here's the even-better part."

I happily sink into a chair, staring up at Dad. "What?"

"My new boss wanted me to live in the castle so I can prepare meals all day. But when I explained that I couldn't leave my family, he offered the cottage house—rent free!"

"A house! For us?"

"It's not a mansion," Dad says with a chuckle. "But there are five rooms. Go out to the computer. The photo is still up. Look for yourself."

I race out of the room to find my sisters waiting for me by the computer.

"Check out our new home!" Kenya gestures with her hand like a model promoting a product.

"Sit here," Kiana adds as she stands up to offer me the chair.

I stare at a photo of a white, two-story frame house surrounded by an orchard and with blooming flowers leading up to the house. The house may be called a cottage—but it's huge! And the yard looks roomy enough for our dog, Handsome, and my kitten, Honey. I can finally take my kitten home! Of course, I'll have to ask my parents, but I know they'll say yes. I can't wait to tell Becca and Leo.

Something else in the photo catches my eye—a gigantic oak tree in the front yard that's taller than the house.

I imagine myself climbing into the tree and peering down from that high perch. Wild animals might come close without knowing they're being watched.

I might even discover a new animal mystery for the CCSC to solve.

Look for more Curious Cat Spy Club mysteries in paperback!

HC 978-0-8075-1376-7 • $14.99 | PB 978-0-8075-1382-8 • $9.99

Kelsey helps catch a runaway zorse with the help of the nicest and most popular girl in school, Becca. The two are walking home when they happen upon a litter of kittens trapped in a dumpster and Leo is the only person around who can help get them out. The three unlikely friends decide to work together to help solve animal crimes with their secret club.

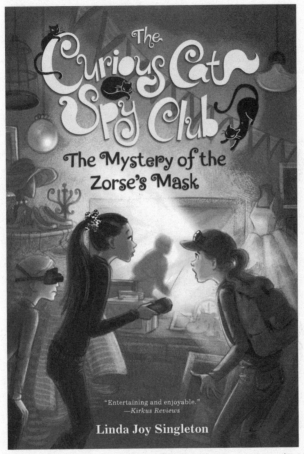

The Curious Cat Spy Club

The Mystery of the Zorse's Mask

"Entertaining and enjoyable."
—*Kirkus Reviews*

Linda Joy Singleton

HC 978-0-8075-1378-1 • $14.99 | PB 978-0-8075-1383-5 • $9.99

When a mysterious stranger claims to own Becca's beloved zorse, Zed, the Curious Cat Spy Club fears he might be responsible for abusing Zed in the past. Kelsey, Becca, and Leo are determined to uncover the truth before they have to give him away. But when a daring rescue attempt puts Kelsey in danger, does the CCSC have enough spy skills to save her, or could the team be in over their heads?

Read on for a sneak peek of the next mystery!

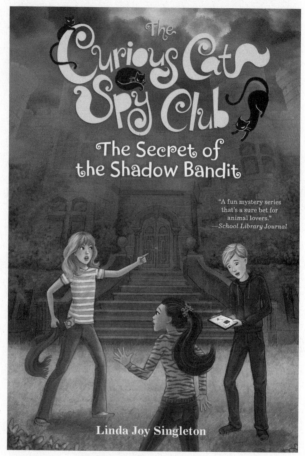

The Curious Cat Spy Club

The Secret of the Shadow Bandit

"A fun mystery series that's a sure bet for animal lovers."
—*School Library Journal*

Linda Joy Singleton

HC 978-0-8075-1385-9 • $14.99

Kelsey's dad has a new job and that means a new house—on the same property as a castle! Kelsey, Becca, and Leo can't wait to explore, but what they find might lead to their most intricate case yet. How are an abandoned tree house, a wad of cash, a missing heirloom, and a mysterious creature roaming the grounds all connected? The Curious Cat Spy Club is determined to find out!

- Chapter 1 -
Monstrous!

A shrill scream rips through the house.

I jump off the window seat, fling my mystery novel aside, race out of my bedroom and —*Wham!*— into the solid mass of big brother.

"Whoa, Kelsey!" Kyle's hair is mussed like he just woke up from a nap. He puts his hands on my shoulders and peers into my face. "Why'd you scream?"

"Not me...Kiana," I say as another scream echoes through the hall. I whirl around and run into my sister's room, my brother close on my heels.

My older sister Kiana is perched on her bed, clutching a stuffed pink bunny to her chest like a shield. "Get the monster out of here!" she shrieks.

"What monster?" Kyle scrunches his forehead, looking around.

"It moved too fast to get a good look, but I think it's a fanged snake or horned lizard with a spiky tail," Kiana says in a rush.

A fanged horned monster with a spiky tail?

I want to believe Kiana because she's nicer to me than Kenya and sometimes she even helps me with my homework. But there's no monster in her room— only the usual mess of clothes, shoes, and makeup my sisters never put away. There are still moving boxes too, even though it's been a week since we moved from our cramped apartment into a two-story "cottage."

"It's in my closet!" Kiana points a shaky finger. "I saw a horrifying shadow on the wall then heard claws running into my closet so I kicked the door shut. It's still there!"

"You only saw a shadow?" Kyle scoffs. "Don't you know that shadows are always more exaggerated than reality? I'm not surprised you're imagining monsters after you and Kenya stayed up late watching *Jurassic Park*."

"That has nothing to do with this...this *creature*!" Kiana squeals, her gaze glued to the closet. "I came into my room to get my backpack and heard a crunching sound—and look! That *thing* chewed my book report!" Kiana picks up a shredded paper from her bed and waves it at us.

I stare at needle-sharp punctures and clawed stripes, and my stomach knots. As Spy Tactics Specialist in the Curious Cat Spy Club, I've trained myself to observe and analyze evidence. The claw and teeth marks are proof I can't ignore. A horrible suspicion grows in my mind.

"A monster ate your homework?" Kyle throws back his head and laughs. "Try getting that excuse by your teacher."

"It's true! And it's probably devouring my clothes and best shoes right now!" Kiana twists a curl of her dark hair around her finger anxiously. "Hurry, Kyle! You're older and stronger than we are. Get rid of it!"

My brother's smile fades fast. While he's tall and can play a mean game of hoops, he's not made of muscles or courage. And lately he's been too busy researching colleges to play any sports. He glances uneasily at the closet, backing into the hall like he's poised for a quick getaway. "I'll go ask Mom to help. Catching animals is her job so she'll know what to do."

"She's working in the garden," Kiana says.

"No need to bother Mom on her day off," I say calmly even though my heart is thudding. I step forward. "I'll do it."

My brother and sister stare at me, shocked. I'm the youngest in the family after all, the little sister who's usually so quiet no one notices me. They probably think I'm trying to prove I can be brave, but my offer has nothing to do with bravery. It's the opposite. If my suspicion about the "monster" is right, I'm going to be in big trouble. My only hope is to get my sister and brother out of the room.

"I can handle this." I visualize I'm a fearless detective from one of my novels and lift my chin confidently. "I've learned a lot about dealing with wild animals from hanging out with Becca at her animal sanctuary. Alligators, lions, and bears—they don't scare me. Becca's taught me how to protect myself, but I can't protect both of you, so wait in the hall."

Kiana frowns at her ripped homework then jumps off her bed and comes over to me. "I can't leave you in here alone," she says.

"Really, it's okay. Don't worry."

As I say this, I hear rustling sounds from the closet and wonder what will happen if I'm wrong.

Could there really be a spiked-tail snake-lizard in the closet?

"Kel knows a lot about wild animals, so she can take care of this," my brother says with a shrug. "Come on, Kiana. Let's get out of here."

"But Kelsey could get hurt." She tugs my hand. "Better my shoes get eaten than my baby sister. Let's all leave and go get Mom."

"Get Mom to do what?"

I spin around as Mom strides into the room. Curly brown hair falls out of her red headscarf and her gardening gloves are dirt-stained. Before she became a county animal control officer, she worked for a florist because she loves gardening.

I wish she'd stayed outside in the garden.

Things get worse when I hear Kenya's and Dad's voices.

Drats! Now my whole family is here.

"What's going on?" Dad squeezes in beside Mom. He must have been in the kitchen working on a culinary masterpiece because he's wearing his *Eating Is a Necessity but Cooking Is an Art* apron.

"Kiana, did you scream?" Kenya pushes past everyone to hug her. They both have long dark-brown hair like Mom's and full lips like Dad, and everyone says they're identical. But I can tell them apart. It's Secret 28 in my notebook of secrets.

"Mom, Dad!" Kiana gestures wildly. "There's a monster in my closet!"

Dad wipes his hands on his cooking apron as he chuckles. "Aren't you a little old for imaginary friends?"

"It's not a friend or imaginary! See what it did to my book report!" Kiana waves her ripped homework in the air. A corner breaks off and flutters to the carpet.

Mom pushes her hair from her eyes, leaning in for a closer look at the paper. "Hmmm," she murmurs. "What does this monster look like?"

"Horrifying! It was huge like a giant lizard or dragon with wicked fangs!" Kiana spreads her arms and juts out her teeth like fangs. "And it had a spiky tail!"

"But you only saw its shadow," I point out, hoping to calm everyone down and convince them to leave. "I'm sure it's just a harmless rat. I can get rid of it."

"No, you will not, Kelsey," Mom says firmly as she steps in front of me. "Rats carry diseases. Kyle, go out to my work truck and grab my net."

We all wait as if frozen in a movie frame. Kiana and Kenya stand close, their hands dramatically clasped together and their gazes fixed on the closet door like they're in a horror movie. Dad stands by awkwardly like an extra, while Mom waits to direct the action.

Minutes later, Kyle's footsteps pound down the hall and he hands Mom the net before he quickly ducks back into the hall.

Mom raises the net in one hand, reaching for the closet with the other.

I hold my breath as Mom twists the knob.

Slowly, the door opens...

- Chapter 2 -
Houdini Cat

"Stand back, kids," Mom warns.

The others huddle in the hall but I step forward to look inside the closet.

Just as I feared, I recognize the "monster."

Of course, there's nothing monstrous about my sweet kitten. Honey is adorable with long marmalade fur, white patches across her back, and a short stubby tail that's twitching now as if she's annoyed.

"Honey!" I rush forward to scoop up my cat. She mews with attitude, letting everyone know she does not appreciate being locked in a closet.

"Some terrifying monster." Mom chuckles, the net dangling from her hand.

Kyle swaggers into the room. "I thought the

monster had a spiked tail."

"It did!" Kiana waves her arms emphatically. "It can't be a kitten!"

"You only saw its shadow." Kyle smirks. "I can't believe you freaked out over an itty-bitty kitty."

"I did not freak out." Kiana glares at him.

"Your scream probably registered on the Richter scale," Kyle jokes.

"You were too scared to even look in the closet." Kiana whirls away from Kyle to point at me, her fear switching to fury. "Kelsey, this is all your fault! Your cat destroyed my homework!"

Uh-oh. Now I have a monster to deal with—my angry sister.

"She's only a kitten and doesn't know any better," I say in a mouse-squeak. Usually Kiana is nice to me, but when she's angry—watch out! Arguing never works. My best strategy is to apologize and beg forgiveness. "I'm really sorry, Kiana. I'll help you rewrite your book report."

"As if a seventh-grader could do high school homework," she harrumphs.

I hug Honey tightly to my chest, not sure which of our hearts is beating faster. "She won't do it again."

"She better not," my dad puts in firmly. "Kittens are too full of energy to run loose in a house—especially a house we're living in rent-free because of the generosity of my new employer. We have to be careful not to damage anything. No stains on the carpet or broken windows or marks on the walls."

I groan. Not another lecture about taking care of our new home. Sure, I'm grateful to Mr. Bragg. (That's King Bragg from the resort hotel commercials with him wearing a crown while skydiving into a luxurious swimming pool.) But Dad is so afraid something will go wrong and he'll lose another job that he's stressing everyone out. It's not like we're toddlers who draw on walls or spill juice on the carpet. Besides, the only reason King—I mean—Mr. Bragg offered us the house was because he wanted his new personal chef nearby to prepare his meals 24/7.

"I assured Mr. Bragg that my family was responsible," Dad continues, not noticing that my siblings have sneaked away. "But Kelsey, I can't allow a destructive animal in this house."

"She's not destructive, just playful," I argue as my kitten bats at my hair.

"And very sweet," Mom adds, stroking Honey's

silky fur. "But I agree with your father. Kelsey, you must keep a close watch on your kitten."

"I will," I assure my parents. "Her litter, food, and water are in my room. I'll make sure she doesn't get out."

"If she causes any more trouble she has to go," Dad warns.

"No!" I hug my kitten to my chest. "Honey won't do anything wrong again. She'll be a perfect little angel. I promise."

I hope this is a promise I can keep.

Dad offers to make tacos for lunch. His tacos are always delicious with his special seasoning and juicy organic tomatoes. I leave Honey in my room curled in her cushioned cat bed.

"You stay right there and don't get into any trouble." I wag my finger at her.

She blinks her golden eyes innocently as if to say, "Cause trouble? Me?"

"Yes, you," I say firmly.

Shutting my door firmly, I hurry downstairs to join my family around the dining table. I plop a taco on a plate and take a big bite. Spicy tomato juice dribbles down my chin and I lick it off. Yum.

When my brother reaches for his third (or fourth) taco, Dad grins. "As the chef, I take that as a compliment. But don't stuff yourself. We have an important dinner tonight." Dad winks as if we need reminding despite him telling us a zillion times about our dinner invitation to Bragg Castle.

It's not really a historical castle but it sure looks formidable with massive stone walls and turrets spiraling to the sky. It's just past a grove of trees beyond our new home. I can't wait to see inside the castle. But I'm kind of nervous too, because King Bragg is famous and I won't know what to say to him. I'm better at listening than talking.

I'll ask Becca for advice. She can talk to anyone. Sometimes I suspect she can talk to animals too, or at least understand what they're saying since she helps her mother run their animal sanctuary. When I called her earlier, she was getting ready to give a bear a bubble bath. Yeah, a real bear.

Becca and Leo, our club's Covert Technology Strategist, will be here in an hour to see my new home. When Dad first told us we were moving into a "cottage," I expected something small and cozy like out of a fairytale. But a five-bedroom house is a cottage to the King of Resorts compared to his castle. I wonder if there will be suits of armor propped up like guards, secret passages, and a dungeon. Exploring a dungeon would be cool.

After lunch, I head up to my room to check on Honey. The door is shut just like I left it. As I step inside, I say, "Honey, I'm back."

She doesn't romp over to rub my ankles or meow to be picked up. And when I look at her kitty bed, only a catnip toy and fuzzy red blanket are there.

My cat is gone.

About the Author

At age eleven, Linda Joy Singleton and her best friend, Lori, created their own Curious Cat Spy Club. They even rescued three abandoned kittens. Linda was always writing as a kid—usually about animals and mysteries. She saved many of her stories and loves to share them with kids when she speaks at schools. She's now the author of over thirty-five books for kids and teens, including YALSA-honored the Seer series and the Dead Girl trilogy. Her first picture book, *Snow Dog, Sand Dog*, was published by Albert Whitman & Company in 2014. She lives with her husband, David, in the northern California foothills on twenty-eight acres surrounded by a menagerie of animals—horses, peacocks, dogs, and (of course) cats. For photos, contests, and more check out www.LindaJoySingleton.com.